# H & G RESTORATIONS

PEPPER NORTH

*Pepper North*
With a Wink Publishing, LLC

Text copyright© 2025 Pepper North®
All Rights Reserved

Pepper North® is a registered trademark.
All rights reserved.

**NO AI TRAINING:** Without in any way limiting the author's [and publisher's] exclusive rights under copyright, any use of this publication to "train" generative artificial intelligence (AI) technologies to generate text is expressly prohibited. The author reserves all rights to license uses of this work for generative AI training and development of machine learning language models.

# AUTHOR'S NOTE:

The following story is completely fictional. The characters are all over the age of 18 and as adults choose to live their lives in an age play environment.

This is a series of books that can be read in any order. You may, however, choose to read them sequentially to enjoy the characters best. Subsequent books will feature characters that appear in previous novels as well as new faces.

You can contact me on
my Pepper North Facebook pages,
at www.4peppernorth.club
eMail at 4peppernorth@gmail.com
I'm experimenting with Instagram, Twitter, and Tiktok.
Come join me everywhere!

## CHAPTER ONE

After turning the H & G truck into the long driveway, Hans stopped to look at the large Victorian house in front of them. It was enormous and picturesque. At least it was as he imagined it could be with a lot of love and hard work. Turrets and quaint windows peered down at them from above as the sagging wraparound porch beckoned them forward. Even in its dilapidated condition, he could see what it once had been.

"This one's going to take a lot of love. Better double—wait, triple the time you estimate. You know we're going to find rot and other problems," his partner and the love of his life, Gretel suggested.

"Noted. Maybe quadruple. Whoever brought us out here must know that this is going to be one hell of a job," Hans predicted.

"Let's go meet him. I've never met a tech wizard before. I wonder what attracted him to the old Candy Lane Mansion. It seemed like it surprised everyone when it sold suddenly."

"I guess we won't ever know sitting here. Looks like he

knows we've arrived." Hans nodded at the large, fit man who had walked out onto the front porch to greet them.

In just a few minutes, the two partners strolled up to the house with their clipboards. Gretel called, "Good morning."

"Good morning!" The deep voice that answered them sent a shiver of delight down Hans's spine. He was committed to Gretel, but they had looked for a special kind of third to complete their pairing for several years. No one had checked off all their boxes, and the duo wasn't willing to settle. It intrigued Hans when he felt Gretel's jolt of interest.

"Sir, I'm Hans and this is Gretel. We're the owners of H & G Restorations. I'll warn you, we're pretty infatuated with this property. It's iconic in Storybrook."

"Hi, Hans. Gretel. I'm glad to meet you. I'm Magnus Scott."

The large man stepped down the creaking stairs. As he emerged from the shadows of the overhanging roof, Hans heard Gretel gasp softly as the sun revealed chiseled features and brilliant, ice-blue eyes. To say he was attractive was the understatement of the century.

"Mr. Scott, it's a pleasure to meet someone invested in bringing this"—Hans gestured to encompass the house—"back to life."

"It certainly needs a bit of work. I was looking around before you got here and put my foot through a floorboard in the kitchen. I'd guess there's some leaking pipes in there," Magnus shared.

"There always is," Gretel piped up.

"My bulk may be a detriment inside until you determine what needs to be done. How about if I stay out here?"

"That's a good idea, sir. We'll get a better idea of what's going on as we move through each room methodically. This will take a while. We could meet you in town late this afternoon to give you the highlights of what we've found. There's no need to hang around out here all day long," Gretel suggested.

When Magnus nodded his agreement, Hans double-checked that he had the right contact number for him. "Where are you staying?"

"I have a place at the Kingston Hotel in town until I can find somewhere to rent for the duration of the remodel," Magnus said. "Perhaps you could meet me there for high tea at four? I've heard it's quite an experience."

"They're usually booked months in advance," Gretel blurted.

Hans could hear the regret coloring her words. She'd asked to do that for a year or so and he hadn't gotten it done.

"Then, it's a good thing I set it up when I booked my room. I'd hoped to have someone to share the tea party with," Magnus explained with a smile at the young woman.

"Thank you, sir. I will look forward to it," Gretel answered, and Hans knew she'd move heaven and earth now to make this dynamic man's house a home. She would have done that anyway, but Gretel loved special connections like this.

"Perfect. I'll leave you to survey the house. You will be very careful, correct? I don't want either of you to take any risks," Magnus said, his voice becoming serious.

"Definitely, sir. We're used to navigating around old houses. We'll meet you with a few scratches, but in fine shape for tea," Hans promised.

"I'll leave you to it."

The two partners watched him walk away. Hans knew he was checking out the handsome man's butt, and following Gretel's line of vision, he wasn't the only one.

"Come on, partner. If we're efficient, we'll have time to shower before we meet Magnus." Hans wrapped an arm around her back to steer Gretel toward their target.

"For high tea!" she said, already celebrating and bouncing beside him in excitement.

"Focus on the work now. You heard Magnus. Be safe."

"Totally dismissing tea to focus," she reported, shuffling through the papers on her clipboard. "I'll head to the basement to check out the foundation, heating, and plumbing."

"I'm coming with you. Until we see the condition of the floors, we stick together," he decreed.

"Aye, aye, sir!" she sassed, saluting.

The swat he landed on her bottom stung his hand slightly, and Hans watched Gretel rub her rear end in surprise. A toot of the luxurious sedan as Magnus turned around made them both realize that their prospective new boss had seen that.

"Hans," Gretel groused as she turned back to stare at the house. "Don't lose us this job."

When he nodded, she grabbed her pencil and pointed upward. "Major roof rot above the porch. All supports and planking need replacing on the front. We'll need to measure for the amount of lumber it will require."

"Agreed."

Cautiously, they made their way through the first floor, taking meticulous notes. Finding the stairs down, Hans descended the steps first to check how they held his greater weight, but also to brush away any spiders that had taken residence inside. Gretel was fine standing in filth as she cleared out the muck of years of plumbing clogs and collapsed pipes, but spiders would give her nightmares that would wake them both.

There was good and bad news on the bottom floor. The foundation was rock solid, but they would need to replace the plumbing and wiring completely. There were a few oddities that puzzled the couple. They recorded everything by taking pictures.

"I'd expected we were going to rewire, anyway. No one who makes their living through technology conquests would be satisfied with the limits of old-fashioned connections," Gretel commented.

The main floor brought its own share of concerns and celebrations. Hans rubbed his hand over the ancient stove that remained in incredible condition for its age. "Do you think he'll want to tear everything out and put a sleek, modern kitchen in here?" he questioned.

"That would be a shame, but it will have to fit the needs of a large man working in here. He'd dwarf this space," Gretel pointed out.

"You noticed how broad his shoulders were too," Hans teased.

"Who could miss that?" She pointed to a large footprint in the dirt next to an even bigger hole smashed through the flooring. "He has to wear a size twice yours."

"Makes you wonder, doesn't it?" Hans teased.

"I am not thinking about our client's personal attributes, other than to note space requirements for a body that... chiseled." Gretel squatted down to probe into the hole Magnus had left. "The subflooring seems pretty solid, but all this has to go. What would you suggest? Room by room or gut the whole thing and start fresh?"

"Save the best and move it into a storage area while we rip up all the rot, rewire and plumb," Hans suggested.

"I agree."

They wrapped up at the bottom of the stairs. It was a gorgeous carved wooden staircase with an intricate pattern that would require hours to strip off the old, gummy varnish and bring it back to life. The couple looked at each other and nodded. This would be totally worth the time to refinish. The craftsmanship couldn't be replicated now.

Armed with a million photographs to show Mr. Scott and their notes, Hans and Gretel climbed back into the truck. They'd have time to clean up if they rushed. Hans noticed Gretel turned back to get another glimpse at the house.

They both felt it. This house called to them for help. And Magnus Scott? He was pure man candy.

## CHAPTER TWO

"Well, you didn't run away so I'm going to consider that a win."

Magnus greeted them with a broad smile that just might have made her heart skip a beat. Gretel watched him signal the waitress that his party was here and marveled at his manners.

She'd done some research on Magnus on their way over, reading tidbits out loud to Hans as he drove. The commanding man didn't come from old money but had done a stint in the military's special forces before leaving to start his own tech support company. He'd carved out a niche for himself in the corporate world and appeared to be well-liked.

The pictures she'd found of him at charity events were intriguing. His companions had featured beautiful females and males of no observable type. She didn't know if he was gay, straight, or bisexual. Claiming a spot between them, Magnus ushered both her and Hans forward into the cozy tearoom with a guiding hand on their lower backs. The heat of his touch radiated through her clothing, and she had to steel herself to not react.

"I'm sorry," he murmured to her, lifting his hand when he felt her stiffen. "Forgive my clumsy attempt to be chivalrous. I think sometimes I was born in the wrong century."

"Oh, no. No apologies needed," she rushed to assure him, seeing Hans look at her in concern. "I was here with my grandmother when I was eight. She was a very big proponent of standing up straight. I almost heard her voice as we stepped into the parlor."

"Ah, grandmothers. They teach us so much. This place does make you feel like you should be on your best manners," Magnus agreed and pulled a chair out for Gretel before surprisingly repeating the action for Hans. Only then did he take his own seat.

The waitress flirted with the two men as she explained how high tea would be served. To Gretel's delight, Magnus was polite and nothing else. When the server departed to gather their drinks, sandwiches, and cakes, he leaned forward to ask, "So, what did you think?"

"There's a lot of work there, sir," Hans shared, pulling out his tablet to show Magnus some of their concerns.

"Call me Magnus for now, please. Talk me through it and then we'll look at pictures."

Gretel ruminated on the strange wording. *What else would they call him?* Forcing herself to concentrate, she added, "There are also treasures that are amazing finds. The stove in the kitchen, the large walnut stairway, and the perfectly preserved stained-glass window in the master bathroom."

"The plumbing and wiring need to be replaced completely. That would allow you to use all the latest technology advances you may wish," Hans pointed out. "We would recommend you pull up the flooring to prevent crashing through again. The subfloor looks good, but we always warn people that we won't know what we'll find as we start the restoration process."

"This will be my first and only home restoration but I'm going into it having been warned by the realtor, my friends, and a cackle of delight from my worst enemy," Magnus shared with a laugh as the server returned with a beautiful display of treats and steaming hot tea.

When she departed, Gretel asked, "Is this house special to you in some way?"

"This is going to sound crazy, but I decided to take myself on an Australian walkabout in my car while not even in that beautiful country. I ended up here and drove past that house. Ignoring the no trespassing signs, I hopped the fence and looked around." Magnus paused to pour himself a cup of tea after carefully serving his guests. After enjoying a few sips, he continued, "Did you know there is a creek that runs behind the house with a deep enough section to cool off on a hot day?"

"How did you know it was deep enough?" Hans asked with a perplexed expression.

"I jumped in. There was a rather large trout in there that wasn't pleased," Magnus confessed. "I promised him I'd make it up to him. So I bought the house."

"You promised a fish and bought a house?" Gretel repeated.

"I did. But only because I fell in love with it. The house, that is. Not the fish," he rushed to assure them before laughing at his own words.

She found herself unable to resist his charm. Laughing, she met Hans's gaze and knew he felt the same. Thank goodness Magnus had passed through.

"What were the weirdest things you found?" Magnus asked.

"Other than super gigantic spiders, most of the rooms were as expected. Small rooms designed to be easier to warm in the winter. This made us both rather curious. Let me show you this one," Hans insisted, swiping through the photos on his tablet.

"Here," he said, handing the device to Magnus.

The large man stared and widened the view to see a bit better. "That looks like a cage."

"Exactly. We're guessing for the family pet? It's a neat, old structure and fairly large. It would be fun to equip with a something unique like a wine rack."

"Like my own private stash. That's fun. There might be some other uses for that. Let's not trash that for now."

"You got it," Hans assured him, noting that Magnus was already talking like they had the job. A nudge from Gretel's foot told him she had perceived the same idea.

Gretel picked up the conversation to assure Magnus, "We'll find more unique treasures. These old houses are always full of secrets. Did you know there was a hidden room off the master bedroom? Hans found it when he moved several exposed wires from the lights. A wall opened."

"A concealed space?" Magnus asked, leaning forward. "What was inside?"

"The passage was jammed. We'll have to work on the mechanism to get it to work. There was something inside that looked like a large crib. It might have just been the angle that made it look bigger than an average crib," Gretel warned, trying to keep her voice even.

"Maybe," Magnus looked intrigued. "It appears that this house called to me for a reason. Let's enjoy this feast in front of us. I didn't know high tea featured such an array of treats."

He picked up the tongs and passed them to Gretel. "Ladies first. Would you clue Hans and me in on what these are?"

"Remember, I was a kid when I did this last. I'd suggest everyone take one of everything and then go back for seconds." She quickly followed her own advice before offering the tongs to her host. When Magnus waved them to Hans, her partner quickly helped himself, following her pattern as Gretel poured more tea for everyone.

The table was quiet for a few seconds as everyone tasted the goodies. Magnus popped a cucumber sandwich into his mouth and groaned his delight. "How can they make something as unexciting as a cucumber into this treat?"

"I remember thinking that as a kid. Who came up with this idea? I'll admit I've tried to make them and my cucumber sandwiches never taste like this," Gretel shared.

"It's probably the complete experience all together—the pretty silver trays, the tea, the special touches. It all combines to make everything taste incredible," Hans suggested.

"And the company," Magnus added, toasting them with his delicate teacup.

It should have looked ridiculous in his hand, but instead, it made Gretel smile. She'd always wanted to have a tea party as an adult with Hans. Having Magnus there made it even more special. She crossed her fingers under the table, hoping with every fiber of her being that they'd get this bid.

The conversation flowed easily around the table. By the time the dessert tray appeared, Gretel felt like they were all comfortable with each other. Clearing her throat, she asked, "Where are you going to stay while your house is being renovated?"

"I'd hoped you could give me some suggestions. I can work anywhere as long as I have high-speed internet. Are there houses to rent around town?"

"I'm sure there are. I can give you the name of a local contact who might have some locations to share," Hans answered.

Magnus smiled and nodded. "I'll take you up on that. For

the time being, I'm here at the Kingston. How long do you expect it to take for you to create an estimate?"

"We'll get it to you this week. I'll give you a hopeful estimate and a dire consequences estimate. It will probably be somewhere in the middle. The subfloor might be bad upstairs or the gingerbread decorations on the gables might be totally rotted. There are a lot of unknowns when renovating an older house. I will give you our promise that we'll discuss any overages with you as we go so there aren't any unpleasant surprises at the end. We will need a deposit to reserve our time and partial payments at various times during the build. I'll detail all that for you," Hans stated.

"Sounds good. Build into your estimate that you check with me if the cost is more than a thousand dollars over the estimate. I don't need to know that you're ten dollars over on light switches," Magnus instructed.

Gretel kept herself from wiggling happily in her chair. He was going to be reasonable. Some jobs were a constant struggle to get approval for overages for even the smallest items. Waiting a week to spend three bucks more for screws could slow everything down to a crawl.

"That would be great. We'll give you an update on any overages on a monthly basis so you'll have that as we work. If at any time you wish to discuss the accounting, we'll set up an appointment to go over all the numbers," Hans promised.

"I'll just ask you this bluntly. I want someone to take on this project because they love the house and want to see it shine once again. Is this just a job for you two or is this your passion?" Magnus asked, deliberately meeting both Hans and Gretel's gazes.

"We love this house. It's an honor to be selected to restore it," Gretel answered enthusiastically. Hans echoed her sentiments.

"Then, it's done. Get me a reasonable estimate that gives me the house I want and gives you a profit that allows your business to continue. I want this to be a win-win situation," Magnus warned them with a grave look.

"Thank you, sir. We appreciate you thinking of us as well. That's a novelty in today's business," Hans answered.

"I'll give you a copy of the floor plans I found online when I bought the house and the ideas for renovations I had created from them by an architect friend of mine. That will help you in the estimate process, I would think?" Magnus proposed.

"Definitely. The original plans were first on my list for tomorrow," Gretel shared.

"Great minds and all that," Magnus said with a smile that made her toes curl up in delight. "Now, let's put all that business behind us. Let's finish our goodies and tea as you tell me about yourselves."

## CHAPTER
# THREE

A week passed in a flurry of activities and calculations. Hans and Gretel helped Magnus get settled in a lovely four-bedroom home located close to the old Candy Lane Mansion. They didn't know why he wanted a home that large, but he'd snapped it up immediately.

Hans and Gretel had run into him several times at the mansion as well as in town. It was if they had the same tastes in stores, restaurants, and bars. Each time, Magnus had chatted with them or invited the duo to join him with a delighted twinkle in his gorgeous blue eyes. There was no debating that he was interested in them—but how?

They were meeting with him this morning with a more detailed estimate than Hans had ever before created. Gretel crossed her fingers as she walked up to his rental home. When he greeted her with a hug, she pushed her shock away that he had pulled her close to his body. She couldn't concentrate on anything other than the feel of his body against hers.

*Damn.*

When he hugged Hans as well, Gretel noted it wasn't one of those back-thumping, boy hugs. Magnus actually pulled him tight in a genuine embrace. Gretel clenched her jaw at the sight of Hans in the older man's arms. It was so hot, checking off all her kinky boxes in her desire to have a third for their relationship. As Hans stepped backward, she noticed he also hadn't been immune from the man's charms.

"Come into the kitchen. I have some goodies set up for you and some milk. I need to keep your strength up."

Hans spread out the original floor plans and the architect's updated design. "This is a brilliant use of all the space you have in the house. There are a few things I'd recommend, but for the main part, we can follow this easily."

Gretel walked Magnus through the largest expenses in creating a stable, healthy home and some upgrades she recommended to make the house more livable. "While we're rewiring, it's easiest to anticipate everything you might need in the future. We automatically put in outlets every three feet. Are you interested in special features like heated floors in the bathroom?"

"Definitely. Let's add some luxury items."

After running through his suggestions to change the architect's plans, Hans answered several questions from Magnus.

"I agree with all your ideas except one. This room accessible from the master bedroom only must remain with the original dimensions. It is an integral part of my lifestyle."

"You lose a lot of space there, sir," Hans pointed out.

"I gain so much more from my nursery," Magnus answered firmly.

"There's enough space in here for four or five infant cribs," Gretel pointed out.

"The room is designed for two special adult Littles to each have their own crib."

Staring at him in disbelief, Gretel clarified, "Littles? Like with a capital L?"

"Exactly. I'd hoped you might understand my lifestyle. That will make it easier," Magnus said, searching her face before checking Hans's expression.

"We weren't expecting that, sir. You'll have to excuse our interest. That's very unique. Of course, you'll need a large nursery close to the primary bedroom. We'll wipe away any ideas to alter that space."

Gretel loved how he tried not to react to Magnus's earth-shattering revelation. He was a Daddy to two Littles. She watched Hans pull his attention away from that thought to refocus on the job at hand. They would have a lot to banter back and forth between them when they were alone.

Finally, it was time to reveal the total. "I prepared two estimates. One bare bones and the other with the best materials and processes." Hans took two sheets of paper from his folder and placed them before Magnus.

Hans dropped his hand under the table to wrap over Gretel's knee and squeeze it. She placed her hand over his and tried to think positive thoughts. They needed this job. The economic conditions had hit H & G restorations hard in the last few years. Without this income, one of them would need to return to some other job to pay their bills.

They were truly on their own. Gretel's stepmother had kicked her out of her father's house when she didn't want any reminders of Gretel's kind mother. Hans's parents had perished in a car accident in his teens. He'd lived with his grandfather for years, learning all he knew from the master craftsman. Gretel had worked along with him to absorb all the skills that seemed to flow through the old man's blood.

"I'm not a bare bones type of guy," Magnus announced as he dismissed one estimate. Tapping the second larger amount, he stated, "I want this to be the home I've always dreamed of having. We'll go with this estimate."

"You realize there could be some variation in our estimate? I always suggest that clients budget an extra five percent on the final total in case they decide to upgrade the countertops or do extensive painting," Gretel warned.

"Got it. When can you start?" Magnus asked.

"We can start next week, sir. Please sign the bottom of the estimate and we'll give you a copy. We'll need half up front to purchase the material, one fourth at the midway point, and the final fourth at the end," Hans informed Magnus, squeezing Gretel's knee in three short, happy bursts.

"I'll give you eighty percent to begin with and the final twenty at the end. If we make changes or run into problems, I'll write you another check." Magnus pulled out his checkbook and his phone to make some calculations. When Hans agreed with the amount he suggested, Magnus quickly wrote out a check.

"Starting next week will allow the check to clear. Is there any other paperwork we need to complete?" Magnus asked.

"No, sir. I think that covers it." Hans extended his hand to shake Magnus's.

"And I am looking forward to you helping the house come alive," Magnus said, shaking Gretel's hand as well. "Now, with all the business taken care of, may I speak to you personally?" Magnus requested.

Hans looked at Gretel before giving him their permission.

"I have looked near and far for my Littles—a Little boy and a Little girl—to have and to hold. If I am completely off base in my suspicion that you are interested in this lifestyle or if you already have a Daddy, will you clue me in to avoid any misunderstandings?"

Gretel scooted a bit closer to Hans, who immediately wrapped an arm around her waist. When he started to answer the dynamic man across the table from him, Gretel whispered, "How did you know?"

"There were small things. The faint, fading imprint of a ring on your mouth at the beginning of the day, Gretel, that appeared to be from sucking on a pacifier. Hans's protectiveness of you that didn't cover his struggle to take that role on completely. My first impression was that you are a bonded pair but you are looking for someone dominant to complete your relationship. Am I off-base?"

Gretel lifted her fingers from tracing her mouth and shook her head.

"I'm wrong?" Magnus asked.

"We don't ever tell anyone. We've never met a Daddy in real life," she whispered.

"Now you have. Will you explore the possibility that we match together as you rebuild my house? Will you allow me to woo you?" the elegant man requested.

"We don't want there to be any unpleasantness if we aren't right for you," Hans hedged. His glance over to Gretel told her he was trying to be professional while controlling his excitement.

"I promise you I will back off completely and only interact on a professional basis if you or Gretel decide I am not a good match for you."

"Okay," Gretel said, whispering once again.

"Thank you, Little girl. And you, Hans?" Magnus asked.

"We are a package deal, sir. No one will tear us apart," Hans answered, lifting their intertwined fingers to rest on the table. Gretel knew Hans wished to make sure that Magnus wouldn't try to make her his only Little.

"I assure you I am extremely attracted to the idea of having a Little boy in my life. I can't wait to find out if you enjoy snuggling on Daddy's lap as much as I hope you do," Magnus revealed.

Gretel watched Hans's face redden with embarrassment. How could Magnus have already figured out that Hans's strong builder appearance disguised his love to cuddle and be loved? "My lap isn't big enough for him," she shared.

"I wouldn't think so, but I'll bet mine is just right. Come let us try it out." He opened his arms and beckoned Hans forward.

When the Little boy froze in place, she recognized that Hans hesitated to expose the truth about himself, fearing scorn. To cover for him, Gretel stood on shaky legs to ask, "Can I go first?"

"Of course, Little girl." Magnus turned his arms to welcome her with a pleased smile.

She walked forward, clinging still to Hans's hand, forcing him to shift closer to Magnus as well. Carefully, she sat on Magnus's thighs, feeling the hard strength below her bottom as she nestled against his chest. An arm wrapped around her waist, holding her securely against his broad chest. Unable to resist, she laid her head on his shoulder after turning to grin at Hans.

"What a delectable lapful," Magnus complimented, giving her a squeeze. "Tell me something about the Little you keep hidden inside."

"I don't like vegetables and I always sleep with Hans and my bunny, Snickers."

"I will look forward to meeting Snickers. I will always ask you to take two bites of whatever is on your plate before refusing to eat anything. Vegetables keep you strong."

Gretel wrinkled her nose and shook her head. "Vegetables are smelly and taste bad," she complained.

"Two bites, little girl. Maybe you'll love my cooking and change your mind."

Gretel couldn't help the skepticism from showing on her face. His chest jiggled under her cheek as he laughed. His hands smoothed over her arm and back, reassuring her.

"Are you a mean Daddy?" burst from her mouth.

"If you mean that there will be rules and consequences for breaking those rules, I am a strict Daddy. I want to keep you safe and happy."

"Consequences? Is that a fancy word for spanking?" Hans asked, shifting even closer.

"Yes. And other punishments," Magnus revealed. "If your tummy hurts and you tell me you feel poorly, I'm not going to place you over my knee for a spanking."

"I'd throw up on your shoes," Hans commented with a grimace.

"Exactly. Going to bed before your bedtime would be more effective. Of course, only after you get some tummy medicine in your bottom."

"In my bottom?" Hans echoed.

Gretel watched him squirm on the seat. The idea of Magnus's intimate care intrigued him. Their play together frequently included this sensitive area.

"Hans likes things in his bottom," she shared.

"Gretel!" Hans protested.

"It wouldn't have been a secret for long. Do you want to share any clues about Gretel?" Magnus asked.

"She's a major grump in the afternoon."

"I am not!"

"You are!"

Magnus laughed and lifted Gretel's chin. Lowering his lips toward hers, he waited for a second to allow her to tell him no.

When she tilted her mouth up silently giving him permission, Magnus kissed her lightly and then again.

He tasted so good—warm, masculine and his own special flavor—totally different from Hans. When he lifted his lips from hers, an involuntary sound of protest escaped from her lips. She wanted more. Looking into his face, she opened her mouth to ask for another and paused when he nodded at Hans. He was right. It was Hans's turn. Gretel leaned back slightly and saw Hans leaning forward as he watched carefully.

Standing with a bit of a wobble, she tugged Hans to his feet. "Sit on Daddy's lap," she ordered.

"We don't know he's our Daddy," Hans hissed into her ear as they swapped positions.

"You will soon," she promised.

He didn't have time to argue with her. Magnus helped Hans sit on his lap. The handsome Daddy wrapped his arms around her best friend and hugged him close. She couldn't hear the words he whispered into Hans's ear, but saw her partner relax.

Hans nodded and leaned forward to press his lips against Magnus's. She watched him try to control the kiss. Magnus returned his kiss but easily changed the power dynamic by tangling his fingers in the younger man's thick, blond hair and holding him in place. Again, Gretel saw the moment Hans yielded to the man wishing to be their Daddy. His shoulders rounded, and he seemed to shrink from the business owner to the Little boy she recognized so well.

"Thank you for trusting me, little boy," Magnus told him after ending the kiss. When he hugged Hans close, he melted against Magnus's broad chest.

Unable to stop herself, Gretel moved toward the two men and wrapped her arms around them both. Magnus skillfully included her in the group hug. Her heart swelled in her chest with happiness. This could be it. They could have found the man they'd given up hope of finding.

Her phone ringing disrupted their shared embrace. Automatically, she shifted to move to it. Magnus held her in place for a fraction of a second before telling her to answer. As Gretel greeted her caller, she smiled. He was already in charge.

## CHAPTER FOUR

Hans didn't know if he was glad Gretel's phone had caused them to have to rush to a different job site to make important decisions or not. With a massive check processing at the bank, Hans had pulled out the contract three times in the twenty hours since they'd left Magnus's house. The sight of the ink signature thrilled him every time.

"Are you ready for the walk-through with the clients today? What do you need me to do?" Gretel asked, interrupting his thoughts. She didn't comment on the document in his hands but rubbed a hand over his shoulders.

"There's a bit of trim in the front bathroom that needs to be fastened into place. It's under the sink."

"I'll take care of it. Would you change the bulb in the entryway light?"

"Of course. Then I plan to walk through each room with a polishing rag and my tools to make sure everything is perfect," Hans shared.

"I'll take the upstairs." His partner jumped in to help as always. "Ready to go?"

Nodding, Hans closed the notebook and placed it on his desk. "Let's get this finished."

As he escorted Gretel from the office he'd commandeered in their apartment, Hans couldn't keep a smile off his face. Magnus's house was a dream job. Replacing the gingerbread and decorations was a treat he desired more than anything else. He loved restoring houses, but bringing this one back to life drew him like nothing had ever affected him. It was almost like that old fairy tale that everyone mentioned upon meeting them. He wanted the mansion to look like it was made of candy. Only this fairytale needed a powerful Daddy instead of an evil witch.

"I'd pay a whole quarter to know what you're thinking about," Gretel teased.

"Oh, it's worth a hell of a lot more than that."

"Really?"

He knew she wanted him to give her details, but he wasn't ready to share all his inner thoughts. Hans squeezed his buttocks together and felt a bit of tenderness between them. They'd experimented with their vibrators last night, imagining Magnus was giving them medicine. He'd come harder than he thought possible and Gretel had screamed her pleasure several times.

Hans sent stern thoughts to his cock as it stirred in his pants and shrugged. He didn't think the well-built man would mind a bit. Magnus definitely wouldn't punish him for it... Or would he? A picture of being stretched naked over Magnus's lap as the large man warmed his bottom flashed into his mind, and Hans groaned with arousal.

"Stop thinking about him, Hans. You can't meet the

Stevensons with a huge boner," Gretel teased, running a fingertip over the bulge straining against his fly.

"You're not helping, brat."

"I'm not a brat. I'm a good girl," she answered with a giggle.

"Right..." He allowed his voice to trail off to reveal his skepticism.

"Hey!"

"I really like him, Gretel. I keep trying to not tumble head over heels. It's so strange. I'm usually the one who keeps their distance."

Gretel wrapped her arms around Hans's neck and squeezed him tight. "You know... It's okay to let yourself fall. I'm right there with you."

Hans pulled her even closer and pressed a kiss on her delicious mouth. She definitely didn't help his arousal. The shy, sweet woman had carved herself into his heart instantly when they'd met. "I shouldn't second guess the attraction between us and Magnus. I knew immediately that you were mine as well."

"Daddy, not Magnus," she corrected.

He nodded slowly. The magnetic man felt right. Hans vowed to take things as they came. Time would tell whether Magnus would earn the title, Daddy.

～

HANS STEERED his truck back to the house in need of saving. The first piles of supplies decorated the lawn along with several dumpsters and trash cans. Gretel hopped out with the order list and got to work checking off the deliveries. He spread the building plans and his schedule of where to start out on a work bench. The crew would arrive in an hour and the site would hum with activity for months to come. These last few minutes to review the plan helped Hans clarify the process in his mind.

"Everything's here, Hans, except for the bags of cement mix you ordered. There's a note on one invoice that those should arrive tonight," Gretel reported forty-five minutes later.

"Perfect. The demolition teams are going to be hard at work today. I'm going to leave the kitchen until last so we can take everything out carefully to see what we can salvage."

"Good plan. I love that stove. If there's any way to restore that, I'll dance with joy."

"We'll do our best." He paused to look down the long gravel drive. Magnus had arrived. Hans had wondered whether he would drop by today. He nodded, drawing Gretel's attention to their visitor as Magnus parked a distance away from the house so he wouldn't be in the way of the workers. They both watched him stroll over to talk to them. Even the way he moved was magnetic.

"Damn, I may be drooling," Gretel whispered.

"Wipe your chin on the back of my shirt," Hans teased. "He'll never notice."

"Hello, H & G Restorations! Are you ready to get started?" Magnus called as he grew close.

"We're in good shape to get the Candy Lane Mansion underway," Hans assured him.

"Of course, you are. I came to grab a kiss for luck before the process starts." Before they could react, Magnus drew them close and tempted them to forget everything with a sizzling kiss.

It felt so good to be in his arms with Gretel smooshed close. *I could so get used to this*, Hans thought before stepping back to regain his equilibrium.

"We'll need to keep our minds focused on the work," he told Magnus, striving for a firm but pleasant tone.

"Gotcha. When do the crews usually work? I'll try to come before or after, so I don't get in the way."

Hans wanted to be amazed that Magnus didn't pull the usual *I'm paying for this—I can stop by whenever I wish* attitude they ran into frequently. This guy just seemed perfect.

"Let us know when you want to come by and we'll walk you around the site for safety. We don't want you falling through the floor again," Hans pointed out.

"I hate to make your day longer, but I hope to see you frequently. Come over for dinner tonight. You can tell me how everything went and I can make sure you eat."

"Deal!" Gretel said quickly.

"It's her turn to cook," Hans shared with a laugh.

"I'll feed you on your day, too," Magnus assured him.

"I'll take you up on that."

"Perfect. I'll take a couple before pictures and get out of here. Would you pose for me by the front stairs?"

A few minutes later, Hans and Gretel looked at each other and grinned as the luxury SUV headed back the way it had come, pulling into the grass to allow the workers to pass as they arrived. The pressure to do well had built up on his shoulders over the weekend. Magnus had added the fun back to the project. Hans knew Gretel felt the same way. He couldn't wait to get started.

## CHAPTER
# FIVE

The front door stood open as they arrived. Gretel hugged herself and peeked over at Hans as he pulled the large construction truck into the driveway. "He knows how to make us feel welcome, doesn't he?"

"Definitely."

She popped open her door as soon as he came to a complete stop. Scrambling out of the tall truck, Gretel rushed up the stairs. The aroma wrapped around her as she got close. *Fresh bread? Who baked bread anymore?*

"Do you smell that?" she whispered to Hans.

"Come in!" Magnus's voice boomed through the screen door.

Looking up, she spotted him framed in the doorway wearing a white chef's apron emblazoned with Kiss the Chef! Gretel laughed and stepped through the door into his arms. She had to do what he said, right?

Panting slightly in reaction to the tantalizing kiss that had taken her breath away, Gretel ran her tongue over the roof of her mouth as the chef embraced Hans just as eagerly. There was no mistaking the flavor that had lingered on Magnus's tongue. Italian! Her favorite.

Hans beat her to it. "You taste amazing!"

"Wait until you take that first bite," Magnus tempted with waggling eyebrows.

"Bring it on. We're starving," Gretel shared.

"Leave your shoes by the door and go wash your hands."

"Yes, sir!" Hans looked like he'd agree with anything to make sure he got to eat. He toed off his shoes and lined them up against the wall as Gretel did the same.

Racing in the direction their host pointed, Gretel jostled with Hans at the door to the bathroom. She washed her hands, eager to get the grime of the day off and even splashed water over her face and neck to remove the grit of the worksite. Grimacing at the dirt she left on the towel on the rack, Gretel regretted that decision.

"It's okay, sweet pea. He won't mind and you feel better." Hans followed her example. After washing and drying his skin, the towel looked even grimier. Slinging it over his shoulder, Hans led the way out of the small washroom.

Gretel followed in his footsteps. She wasn't going to let Hans eat everything before she got some.

"Sorry, Magnus. We got the towel grimy. I can take it home and wash it," Hans offered, taking responsibility.

"No way. I'm glad you made yourself at home. Go throw it in the washer," Magnus directed, waving his hand toward a door off the kitchen. "Then, come sit down."

Gretel hesitated at the table, not sure where to sit.

"Either on my left or my right, Little girl."

Magnus allowed her to choose. Next to each of the table settings was a folded piece of fabric. One was decorated with teddy bears and the other with bunnies. Instantly, she headed for the one on the right. As she slid into her seat, she traced a finger over one pair of long ears.

"I thought you'd like the bunnies," Magnus commented as he reached over her shoulder to pick up the material and unfold it.

"You're over there." Gretel pointed to help Hans when he returned. She froze when Magnus wrapped the protective cloth around her neck and fastened it.

*A bib?* She waited to see Hans's reaction before she said anything.

"I don't want you to get sauce all over yourself," Magnus confirmed her silent guess as he secured the teddy bear one.

To her surprise, Hans didn't make a silly joke or refuse to wear it. He simply glanced to double check that the front door was now secure and that no one could see into the kitchen windows. Magnus sat down between them and held out his hands to each side. Automatically, Gretel and Hans placed their palms against his.

"Thank you for joining me for dinner tonight. At my evening meal, I always celebrate something special that happened in my day. I'll invite you both to join my tradition by sharing a great memory from your day," Magnus explained.

"Today, two incredible professionals began working to bring my new home back to life. I am so excited to see what happens to it," he told them with a meaningful glance to both guests.

Hans nodded at Gretel signaling her to go next. She cleared her throat and announced, "I pulled down a bunch of spiderwebs and avoided getting insects in my hair."

Once it was out of her mouth, Gretel felt silly. Why had she chosen that to share?

"Ugh! I would not like to have eight-legged animals

crawling around on my head. That is indeed something to celebrate," Magnus commented, squeezing her hand.

"It's silly," Gretel mumbled, peeking up at him.

"Nothing that brightens your day is silly," Magnus assured her with a smile.

"I don't want any spiders in my hair either," Hans agreed before adding sadly, "That usually happens at least once or twelve times a day. I wasn't as lucky as you today."

"Tell Magnus what you found!" Gretel suggested.

"Definitely, that was my fun for the day. I pulled down a section of wall to check out the wiring and found a bunch of old recipes. The names were strange: gingerbread shingles, peppermint windows, fudge stepping-stones, and a few more."

"Sounds like someone's recipes for a house made of sweets," Magnus said with a delighted grin. "I wonder how they ended up in the walls?"

"I scooted a kitchen cabinet out to get to the wall. There was a gap in the wallboards. Maybe they just slid in there?" Hans suggested. "We find a lot of strange things inside older houses: newspapers, photos, etc. I have a box I stow things the owner might like to keep."

"That will be a magic box. Thank you for taking care of the special treats you come across. I'll look forward to seeing all the surprises inside," Magnus enthused.

"That's much better than my spiders," Gretel whispered under her breath.

"This isn't a competition, little girl. The smallest—or in your case, avoiding the smallest—things can make a tremendous impact on your day. That's incredibly important. Thank you both for celebrating something from your day," Magnus said before asking, "How about something to eat?"

"It smells amazing," Hans said, sitting up straighter.

Magnus reached forward to open a large casserole dish

sitting in the center of the table. Setting the lid aside, he picked up Gretel's plate and placed a piece of chicken smothered in sauce and cheese on one side and a healthy serving of spaghetti on the other. He set it in front of her.

"Thank you. Mmm," Gretel said, leaning over her plate to sniff the delicious scent.

"You're welcome."

Dishing up a second plate, Magnus placed it in front of Hans before fixing his own. "Oh, fiddlesticks! I forgot the bread. Eat, little ones, while it's hot. I'll be back in a second."

Gretel didn't move to pick up her fork. It seemed rude to eat without their host. She leaned back over to sniff again and jumped when Magnus's hand smoothed over her back.

"Eat, Gretel. You're hungry. Here's a breadstick," he encouraged, setting a long golden-brown piece of bread on her plate.

Immediately, she lifted it to her mouth and hummed with delight. "Yum!" she mumbled as she chewed.

"I'm glad you like it." Magnus kissed the top of her head before adding in a whisper, "Don't talk with your mouth full, sweetness. I don't want you to choke."

Silently celebrating the delicious taste, she wiggled happily in her chair as she devoured the treat. It was easy to taste that this wasn't frozen from a box and full of chemicals. He had crafted it from scratch—for them.

Magnus placed another on each of their plates without a comment. Gretel looked over to see Hans popping the last bite of his first into his mouth. He loved them, too. She saluted him with a wave of her treat.

When the dynamic bread maker rejoined them at the table, she swallowed carefully and said, "You're spoiling us."

"That's what Daddies do. Try the spaghetti. Littles can't live on breadsticks alone."

"I could," Hans volunteered cheerfully before swirling his fork in his pasta and trying it. His smile of approval said it all, so Gretel dived in.

Magnus filled the silence as they took the edge off their hunger with the first few bites. "I had a great day as well. After visiting the house, I drove around the area to get a feel for my new neighborhood. I ended up at a farmhouse to the west. They were very friendly and glad to hear that the house was getting a makeover. I heard some great things about you two as well."

"Nice. Was that the Sullivans?" Hans asked.

"Yes. They said you'd done some work for them on a guest cottage. You did such a great job their aunt had decided to stay. They forgive you, though."

"That's amazing. I wouldn't have left either. The design was completely charming," Gretel said with a big smile. The combination of knowing their hard work was appreciated as well as the delicious food made all their efforts worthwhile.

"Another H & G positive review!" crowed Hans.

"I hear a lot of those. You two have made quite an impression on the community," Magnus complimented.

"That's the biggest win. We wanted to build a positive reputation in the community," Gretel shared.

"I got the impression that I'd benefitted from hiring you two as well. It seems that everyone believes I must be a smart cookie to have chosen your company," Magnus shared. "Thanks for making me look good."

"You'd look good anywhere," Gretel said before realizing that her words could be taken for more than just a compliment on his intelligence. She felt her cheeks heat and knew she was blushing. Quickly, she concentrated on her plate, hoping neither man read into her words.

Magnus didn't comment, but simply wrapped his hand

over hers and squeezed reassuringly. She peeked up at him and found him smiling.

"Eat, little girl."

Feeling less self-conscious, she took another bite. Gretel let the two men's conversation waft over her as she relaxed and enjoyed her food. With her hunger satisfied, weariness crashed over her. A big yawn escaped her control and she quickly covered her mouth, hoping her host hadn't seen.

"Finish your food. Then it's bath time and bed for you," Magnus declared.

"That sounds heavenly, but I have a few things to plan before bed," she confessed.

"Everything can wait until tomorrow. Look at Hans. He's as tired as you are. I bet if you go to bed, he will as well."

"I'm wiped too, Gretel. We tackled some big chores today." Hans set his fork down to rub a hand over his face. "I'm sorry, we'll have to head home soon."

"I think you're too exhausted to drive home safely. I have plenty of room. You can shower and crash here. I'll throw your clothes into the washer and you will have them fresh for tomorrow," Magnus decreed.

"Oh, we couldn't impose on you," Gretel rushed to refuse nicely.

"You're doing me a favor. I get more time with you. I'll go start the bath with bubbles. There's room for you both. What time do you need to get up?" Magnus questioned. Waving off their protests after Hans named a ridiculously early time, Magnus set his napkin down and strode from the room to set the alarm and start the water in the tub.

"We can't stay, right?" Gretel asked Hans. She really wanted to spend more time with the man she thought could be her Daddy. How would they know without being around him as much as possible?

"I didn't know how tired I was, Gretel. You'd have to sing to me all the way home to make sure I didn't fall asleep behind the wheel."

"Then we stay. A bath sounds so good. You'll take one with me?"

"My back is doing somersaults at the thought of soaking in a warm tub."

"Perfect. The water is warming," Magnus announced as he returned to the kitchen. "Are you finished eating?"

"Yes, sir," Hans answered. "It was delicious."

"I'm glad. And you, little girl? Do you want another bite?"

"No way. I'm stuffed. Thank you for feeding us," Gretel said, pushing her chair back to stand. "We'll do the dishes."

"You'll carry your plate to the kitchen and set it on the counter. That will help your Daddy. Then it's off to the bath for you." Magnus shooed them down the hallway, promising to come grab their clothes for the laundry and bring them something to wear to bed.

Gretel followed the sound of the pouring water. Walking through the master bedroom, she discovered a huge bathtub. A groan of delight whispered from her lips and she pulled her shirt over her head and unfastened her pants. Eager to wash the grime of the day off, she finished undressing in record time and stopped to potty quickly before turning off the water and getting in the tub.

Hans followed her almost immediately. As he settled against the opposite end, he stretched out his long legs with a groan of contentment. "This is heaven." Scooping up an armful of bubbles, he smoothed them over his chest.

"Don't hog all the bubbles, Hans!" Gretel protested, gathering a mound against her chest.

"Littles, share!" Magnus directed as he stepped into the bathroom with a smile. "That looks like fun. Let me throw these clothes into the washer, and I'll bring you some clothes to put on when you get out."

When he left, Gretel looked at Hans. "On a scale of one to ten, how much do you think he's our Daddy?"

"Twelve."

"Me, too. I don't know how I know. I just do," she agreed with an enormous yawn. Closing her eyes, she melted against the back of the tub.

## CHAPTER SIX

A whisper of movement made her crack her eyelids open. She watched Magnus set a small pile of clothes on the vanity before he knelt by the side of the tub close to Hans. Dipping a fluffy washcloth into the water, Magnus smoothed it over the younger man's shoulder and up his throat.

"Close your eyes, Hans," he directed and washed the perspiration and dust away that coated his face. "Dip your head under the surface, little boy. You have all sorts of things in your hair."

As Gretel watched Magnus lather thick shampoo through Hans's short, blond hair, she battled jealousy and happiness that their Daddy had started with Hans instead of her. Those strong fingers rubbed over Hans's scalp, cleaning his hair and drawing a moan of delight from his lips. She could almost feel Magnus touching her. Gretel wiggled her fingers in the water in anticipation.

As Hans ducked his head under the faucet to wash away

the suds frum his hair, Magnus told her quietly. "He needed me to touch him first, sweetheart."

She nodded immediately. Magnus was right. As they'd talked about having a Daddy, Hans had worried most that someone would be attracted to Gretel and simply tolerate him. Hans needed to know that Magnus wanted him as much as he wanted Gretel. "It's okay. There's two of us. Someone has to go first."

"It's your turn next time to be first," Hans suggested as he sluiced the water from his face and hair. "Damn, that feels better."

"Language, little boy."

"Golly gee whiskers, that feels good," Hans joked.

"Much better," Magnus approved, as he rubbed the washcloth over Hans's back.

Gretel watched the expressions change on Hans's face as the handsome older man washed him. She could see relaxation and sexual tension battle in his expression as Magnus touched him. The water distorted her view, but Gretel could tell that his cock had responded eagerly. When Magnus's hand disappeared under the water to wash his abdomen, the younger man's eyes rolled back in his head. Unable to resist, she scooted closer.

"Uh, uh, Gretel. This is Hans's turn. Daddy will come to wash you soon."

At the sound of his firm tone, Gretel moved back to her side. She'd follow his instructions—this time. Peering through the bubbles and sudsy water, she watched the white washcloth wrap around Hans's cock and stroke up and down repeatedly, pulling a low groan from her best friend's lips.

"Bend your knees and spread your legs wide, little boy," Magnus directed as he moved the cloth. "I'll need to get every nook and crevasse to make sure you're clean, Hans."

Gretel thought about scooting down under the water to watch but knew the soap would burn her eyes. Unable to tear her gaze away from the water rippling against Hans's chiseled abdomen, she pushed her shoulders back against the tub wall. Without a deliberate thought, her hands glided over her stomach to trace the cleft of her pussy. The slickness already gathering there despite the water eased her fingers through the pink folds. She shivered as she guided one fingertip over her clit.

"You don't have to clean there," Hans protested weakly, drawing her attention back to the couple on the other side of the tub.

"Of course, I do. You need to be clean everywhere. Relax your bottom, little boy."

The low moan that followed told Gretel that Magnus had persisted successfully. She watched the older man draw his hand firmly from the root to the tip as he attended to Hans's bottom. It didn't take long. Hans moaned his climax into the warm room as his hips thrust against that arousing touch.

Gretel's fingers worked furiously between her legs, trying to finish before Magnus noticed what she was doing. Somehow, she knew he wouldn't approve.

"Little girl."

She froze, feeling as if she were only a few touches away from reaching her own pleasure.

"Arms crossed over your chest," Magnus ordered in a tone that didn't allow her to refuse.

On edge, she watched Magnus soothe Hans, helping him descend from his orgasm. When Hans rested limply against the tub, Magnus quickly washed his legs, feet, and toes. To finish, he stretched the warm washcloth over the younger man's chest like a blanket and leaned over him to kiss his lips lightly.

"Thank you, Daddy," Hans whispered.

"You're very welcome, little boy."

"Gretel has been very good," Hans informed him.

She wiggled her toes under the cover of the water in appreciation of Hans turning the spotlight on her. When Magnus turned to look at her, she looked down at the surface of the water, feeling suddenly shy and insecure. Maybe he didn't want to touch her like he had Hans.

"You have been very good, Gretel." He caressed a damp hand over her cheek to cup her chin, raising it until their eyes met. "It had to be exciting to see your Daddy touching Hans."

Gretel nodded eagerly before confessing, "I knew I shouldn't touch myself, but I couldn't... not."

"There's nothing wrong with caressing yourself, little girl, if you have permission. Did you ask Daddy if you could make yourself feel good?"

"No," she answered softly.

"Why do you think I told you to stop?"

"Because you wanted to make me feel good yourself?" she asked hopefully.

"Exactly. You've been very patient waiting for your turn. Are you ready for me to touch you?"

"Please," she said breathlessly as the air seemed to evaporate inside her lungs.

Picking up a fluffy new washcloth, Magnus dipped it into the water and cleaned her face and neck, making Gretel groan with delight. It felt so good to have him wash away the grime of the day. So much better than doing it herself! The soft cloth spread over her collarbones and whisked over the swell of her small breasts before its progress halted.

"Dip your head under the water, sweet girl. Your hair needs to be cleaned, too." He smoothed a hand over her hair before unfastening the elastic band at the tail of her braid and releasing her tresses.

Eagerly, Gretel slid her bottom so she could lean back in the tub, lowering her head under the water. When she sat up, he wiped the liquid from her eyes before pouring shampoo into her hair and working the lather across her scalp and to the ends. She would have been happy to sit there forever, basking in his attention, but Magnus had her dunk her hair under the faucet to rinse the suds away. She'd never seen a faucet set in the middle of the tub. It was convenient for her and Hans, and she made a mental note to discuss changing the placement of the faucets in the Candy Lane Mansion restorations with him and Magnus.

"That feels better, doesn't it? Let's get your skin all clean, too."

Gretel nodded eagerly and closed her eyes to hide her excitement as he picked up the washcloth to continue. He smoothed it over her arm and down to her fingers, paying attention to each digit and smoothing the tension from a day of holding power tools before treating the other arm with as much care. The lap of the water against her torso made her hope that he'd wash her chest next. When he glided the material around her small breasts, she sucked air into her lungs in response to the sizzling reaction of his touch on her sensitive mounds. The flick of his thumb over her taut nipples made her bite her lower lip to control the groan that threatened to reveal her reaction.

"Let Daddy and Hans hear your sounds, babygirl. We need to know how you're feeling," Magnus instructed patiently.

"Yes, Daddy," Gretel whispered, unaware that she'd automatically called him by that title.

He cupped her jaw to praise her. "I like hearing you say that, Gretel. Call me Daddy again, please."

"Daddy? Can you wash me lower?" she asked.

"That's my eager Little girl." Catering to her, he stroked over her tummy and the soft mound between her legs.

Gretel's breath caught in her throat, and she shifted her legs apart to encourage his exploration. To her dismay, he swept over her thighs and down to her toes. She wiggled her toes in protest as he cleaned between them before carefully washing her legs. When he dropped the washcloth into the water, she looked at him in protest.

"But..."

"Daddy's not done, little girl. I need you to kneel in the water."

Magnus helped her move into position. Gretel felt very exposed to his view as well as Hans, who watched very closely. When Magnus asked her to loop her arms around his neck, she clasped her hands behind his head eagerly and shivered as his hands slid over her back to cup her bottom.

"That's my good girl," he praised, lifting one hand from her skin.

She heard the soft sound of the liquid soap he used before she felt his remaining hand part her buttocks. The slick mixture made her shiver as he spread it between her cheeks. He circled a fingertip around that small entrance hidden between them before pressing inward slightly. The combination of him stretching that tight ring of muscles and the burn of the soap on her inner tissues made her groan in arousal. She knew he had done this to Hans as well and clenched her inner thighs together as her arousal grew.

"Nothing is off-limits to your Daddy, Gretel. Someday, I'll make love to you here just as I'll make love to Hans's bottom. Do you think you'll like having me inside your tight passage?" Magnus forced her to focus on his words as just his fingertip glided in and out of her body.

"No," she lied, more turned on than she could remember

ever being. Being forced to accept Magnus's attentions while her lover watched pushed the sexual tension to increasing levels.

*Whack!*

The sting of his sharp swat on her bottom made Gretel jerk her bottom forward. "I'll be good," she promised.

"Good Little girls don't lie to their Daddies. Does it excite you to think about me inside your tight bottom?" he repeated.

When she didn't answer immediately, another sharp slap landed on her skin. "Okay! Yes! It makes me hot."

"It makes Hans hot, too."

Gretel's gaze shot to Hans, whose hands clasped the top of that washcloth draped on his chest. His deep blue eyes devoured the scene in front of him. As she met Hans's gaze, she felt Magnus's finger slip from her and his hands rinse the soap from her bottom. That tantalizing touch moved to trace the crease of her pussy. She knew he could feel how hot she was and hid her face against his shoulder.

"I've got you, little girl," he assured her. "It's okay to need your Daddy's touch."

She closed her eyes as his touch pressed into her pink folds. He seemed to read her mind, touching her with just the right pressure in all the most sensitive places. When he entered her with one thick finger, she groaned with delight and bounced slightly on top of him. Gretel needed more.

"Please?" she begged and gasped when he replaced one finger with two to stretch her. "Yes!"

"I think it's time for you to come now, little girl." When she nodded her head in complete agreement against him, Magnus rotated his hand to brush his thumb over her clit.

Holding her breath, she felt those incredible tingles gathering together. She slid her hands down to tighten on his shoulders as she pressed kisses onto his skin. In a flash, her body shook as the approaching climax crashed over her. Her kiss became a bite as she tried to tether herself to his stable form. He reassured her with soft words and caresses to her body with his free hand as he coaxed sensations deep inside her.

When his fingers finally slid from her tight channel, she slumped against him. He smoothed water over her pussy. That light touch sent tremors through her, making her shiver against him.

"Let's get you out of the tub, sweet little. I don't want you to catch a cold." Magnus stood and helped her out of the water. Wrapping her in a thick towel, he towel-dried her hair before turning to repeat the process for Hans.

Within a few minutes, he had them both dressed for bed and brushed out their hair. Gretel loved that he held a hand against her head as he untangled her long hair to avoid tugging it painfully. He always seemed to think of how he could be nice to her. She wasn't used to being spoiled.

"Brush your teeth and go potty," Magnus directed after allowing them to choose their favorite color from the new toothbrushes he had in a drawer. "I'll be right back. I'm going to change the wash so your clothes will be dry tomorrow."

When he disappeared from view, Hans whispered, "Is this actually happening? He seems too good to be true."

"I'm not going to pinch myself in case this is a dream. I don't want to wake up."

"Me, neither. I can't believe this."

After rinsing her mouth, Gretel dashed into the toilet area before Hans and then waited for Magnus to reappear. When her partner rejoined Gretel, she leaned against him for support. Hans wrapped an arm around her and pulled her close before pressing a soft kiss on her temple.

"You were hot in the bathtub," he reported.

"So were you. I tried to... you know."

"I saw. That was exciting as well. I enjoyed knowing that you were turned on as well," Hans admitted.

"You were good. You didn't try to touch yourself."

"No way. Especially when I saw him spank you."

"I kinda liked it," she confessed.

"You know a punishment spanking will be much more intense."

"I know," she answered meaningfully.

"Where do you think he'll have us sleep?" he whispered, changing the subject as he adjusted his thickening shaft in his borrowed sleep pants. She understood he needed to think about something else.

"You'll sleep with Daddy." The magnetic man's deep voice came from the doorway, making them whirl around.

"Really?" Gretel squeaked.

"I want you close to me. Come get into bed."

After escorting them to the big bed in the main bedroom, Magnus requested, "Choose a number between one and one hundred."

"Forty-seven," Hans said quickly.

"Seventy-five," Gretel announced, using her best strategy.

"It was sixty-three. Gretel, you win. You get to choose—next to Daddy or on the edge."

"Daddy," she announced immediately before looking at Hans to make sure that was all right with him.

"Just plan on being a Daddy-Hans sandwich," Hans warned.

"I can handle that," she promised before yawning widely.

"In the middle, sweetness. Hans in next," Magnus decreed and tucked the covers around them both when they had settled into place.

Stretched out on her tummy and feeling snug where

Magnus had settled her, Gretel couldn't see much of their new Daddy as he moved around the room getting ready for bed. From the irregular breathing coming from Hans, he put on quite a show. She was almost asleep when he crawled into bed and pulled her close to his bare chest. Hans snuggled behind her. Warm, exhausted, and protected, she crashed into sleep.

# CHAPTER SEVEN

Armed with a breakfast sandwich and a small cooler with sandwiches and who knew what else, Gretel and Hans set off for their day in a rush to get to the site before their team made it there. Their clean clothes even smelled fresher than normal. Magnus just made everything better. He was, however, hard to leave as he waved goodbye in those droopy sleep pants that revealed everything.

"This cuts fifteen minutes off our drive and we get breakfast," Hans pointed out with a grin.

"I slept well," Gretel shared. It had been like heaven cuddled between the two men. She'd woken up to sweet caresses from two different sets of hands during the night.

"Me, too. I feel like I can do anything today. I think I'll investigate the roof. We've got some clear days stretching ahead of us. I bet we can get the shingles off. With new gingerbread trim, this house will tempt us to eat it!"

"Ugh, now you are buying into the Hansel and Gretel fairy tale," Gretel said.

"Maybe it's true."

"That story didn't end well. The witch threw Hans into a cage and tried to fatten him up to eat him," Gretel pointed out.

"So, he's a mesmerizing wizard instead of a witch and he did make parts of me grow bigger," Hansel pointed out with a sly grin.

"And eat could have a whole new secondary meaning," Gretel pointed out.

"Wow, you think dirty in the morning."

"Magnus made appointments for us to have some tests done in the next town over. You go today at one. I go at four," Gretel told him. "He's going at ten. I sent you an invite with the address of the center and Magnus's address. We'll have them send the results there."

"He's not messing around, is he?"

"Daddies take care of everything I guess? It's easier for us to zip out to an appointment and pick up some stuff while we're away from the site. I know you and I are okay."

"I can't wait for us to be together... you know, really together," Hans stated as he turned into the driveway of the waiting house. "If I get done fast, I'll stop and get both of us some clothes. No one will say anything today, but if we keep wearing the same jeans and T-shirts, day after day..."

"Every crew we have will eventually notice," Gretel ended for him.

"Yep. If I don't have time, you stop on your way back," he suggested.

"That works. Just bring that stack of clean clothes on my dresser that I never put away. I like all those things."

"Magnus isn't going to like your messiness," Hans predicted. "Maybe he'll put you in the cage in the basement. He didn't want to get rid of that, remember?"

A sizzle went through her as she slid out of the car and Gretel forced her mind away from his suggestion. To give herself time to recover, she chewed the last bite of the delicious food Magnus had sent with her before announcing, "I'm working on the living room floor today. I'm going to pull up the boards to put in a new subfloor before we add new flooring."

"Go, team!" Hans joked as they separated to greet the teams working with them today.

∽

WHEN THEY PULLED up at Magnus's rental at the end of the night, Gretel was dragging. She'd taken time off to run to the clinic for the testing Magnus had scheduled after cleaning up the best she could with a bottle of water. Gretel was always used to working hard but today's job had challenged even her endurance. Every muscle in her body was starting to hurt. Easing herself out of the truck, she noticed Hans moved slowly as well.

"We're getting old," she ribbed her partner.

"Definitely. The first days are usually the hardest with all the demolition. Then the fun stuff starts when we get to put it all together," he reminded her as he wrapped an arm around her waist to help her up the stairs to the door.

"You're moving slow tonight. Hot bath or shower?" Magnus asked to greet them.

"Shower. I think I have a thousand dead critters in my hair from pulling up the flooring," Gretel said with a grimace as she stepped out of her shoes in the entryway.

"Good plan," Magnus said, closing the door behind them. "Dinner can wait for a few minutes while you both get cleaned up. Clothes in the washer. No need to scatter critters around."

Laughing, he steered them into the laundry room. As he stripped off Gretel's T-shirt, he observed, "We need to look at those house plans. It would be handy to have the laundry room next to one of the entrances so I can help you shuck off your dirty clothes as you walk in."

Hans met Gretel's gaze, and she knew he was thinking the same thing. Magnus planned on keeping them. He was designing the house with them in mind. Not just any two Littles.

"Don't look so surprised. You hadn't figured out that I wasn't letting you escape?" Magnus asked with an indulgent smile.

"You haven't known us for too long," Hans said, pulling his shirt over his head.

"Let me help you, little boy," Magnus reprimanded him gently as he brushed Hans's hands away from his jeans. "Critters get priority."

"Thank goodness," Gretel said as Magnus returned to unfasten her jeans and draw them down to the floor so she could step free.

He remained kneeling on one knee in front of her to strip off her socks. When his fingers hooked into the sides of her panties, she held her breath. She loved having all his attention on her. This felt so intimate to have him remove her clothing. His hands smoothed over her bare bottom and down her thighs as he removed the scrap of lace.

"Hans, help Gretel with her bra, please," Magnus requested as he rotated slightly to unfasten Hans's jeans.

Gretel loved Hans's eagerness as he traced his hands over her shoulders and down her arms before reaching around her to unhook her bra. They'd been together for a couple of years. To her delight, his desire to see and touch her hadn't dampened. Hans still looked at her with that same hungry expression she'd seen their first time together.

"Okay, little ones. Time to get clean," Magnus announced, standing up between them. "Showers now."

He ushered them naked through the quiet house and into the main bathroom. Gretel looked longingly toward the tub but forced herself to head into the walk-in shower. To her delight, she found the large space contained two shower heads. They wouldn't have to share. After testing the water temperature of one with her hand, Gretel stepped under the warm deluge, dipping her head under the spray to claim it as hers.

"In you go," Magnus urged Hans into the large shower space as well. When he took his place under the other cascade of water, Magnus warned, "No play without Daddy. Get all the yuckies of the day washed away and come to the table. I'll set robes out for you."

As Gretel washed her hair, she caught glimpses of Magnus bustling around the bathroom. She sighed in relief as the suds washed down the drain. A tomboy through and through, Gretel loved her work, but getting stuff in her hair was over the line for her.

Peeking at Han's body, she appreciated his powerful form. He worked hard every day, and those chiseled muscles were honestly earned. She reached out to smooth a finger over a blooming bruise on his upper thigh. "That had to hurt."

"I was just glad I had time to move before the board came down to whack me in a much more sensitive spot." Hans replayed his moves and she could anticipate where he could have gotten hit.

"A bruise there wouldn't have been fun," she agreed.

"Look at all of these." Gretel pointed to deep scratches on her upper arm.

"I bet that hurt, too," Hans commiserated.

"Finish up, little ones. I want to treat your booboos before dinner," Magnus said from the open doorway.

"Just a minute," Gretel called. She quickly finished

cleaning her skin and rinsing the conditioner out of her hair. She squeezed the excess moisture from her tresses before stepping forward into the bright blue, fuzzy robe that Magnus held open for her. The soft fabric felt amazing on her skin and she rubbed her cheek on the fuzzy material covering her shoulder.

Looking up, she spotted Hans wearing an emerald-green robe that made his deep blue eyes look more like the ocean. It was the perfect color choice for the handsome blond. How could he have known what their favorite colors were?

Magnus pushed up her sleeve to examine the scratches on her arm. "Hmmm, little girl. You need to be more careful."

"I was wearing gloves. Things just shifted and got me."

"Accidents happen. That's why they're called accidents and not on purposes. Just be sure to tell me and we'll treat them, okay?" he asked, looking deep into her eyes.

"Okay." Gretel liked him taking care of her. She could have done it all herself but having him smooth on antibacterial ointment and a wrap of gauze for the evening felt nice. "I could get used to this."

"That's the plan," Magnus said with a wink.

"I'm starving!" Hans said from the doorway where he'd been watching.

"Let's go."

Tonight's dinner was a creamy cheese and potato soup. It was absolutely delicious and so easy to eat, even though they were almost falling asleep at the table. Magnus gently pulled the spoon out of Hans's hand and lifted a portion of the thick mixture to his lips when the younger hand propped his cheek on his hand to stay seated upright at the table. To Gretel's amazement, Hans let their Daddy feed him. He even leaned against the older man's powerful frame for support as he struggled to stay awake.

When the bowl was empty, Magnus instructed them to prepare for bed. "You're both asleep on your feet."

"It's way too early. We wanted to look at the floor plans. Any changes need to be made soon," Hans mumbled.

"Tomorrow morning will be soon enough. You need to be in bed, little boy."

Hans rubbed his hand over his face and nodded. "Sorry. I'm not being a very exciting Little for you. I just eat and sleep."

"And let me take care of you. I understand you are busy and I'll insist you take some time to relax and restore your energy. For tonight, it's bedtime," Magnus pronounced. He stood and tugged Hans to his feet.

"And you, little girl. You're just as tired. Are you sleeping next to Daddy tonight?"

"It's Hans's turn," she mumbled reluctantly.

"And then yours tomorrow," Magnus reminded her. He ushered them into the bathroom to brush their teeth and then to bed.

"I'm not that tired," Gretel tried to convince him. The gigantic yawn that followed her assertion proved her to be a liar.

"In bed, little girl. Tomorrow, we'll spend more time together," Magnus promised.

She was almost asleep before he tucked the covers delicately under her chin and tightly around their bodies. "I'm a Gretel burrito," she mumbled as she wiggled to find the perfect spot.

His chuckle rumbled over her, making the corners of Gretel's mouth tilt upward in amusement. She felt his lips brush tenderly over her lips and then at that sensitive spot behind her ear. Gretel sighed in contentment.

"Sleep now, sweetness. Tomorrow is another day together," Magnus promised.

"*Mañana*," Hans corrected. He must feel like a burrito, too.

The bed dipped under Magnus's weight as he sat on the empty space. "Let me read you a bedtime story. I have an entire book of different fairy tales."

He began reading and Gretel tried to concentrate on his words. Soon, his beautiful voice faded away as her dreams took over. She crashed into sleep, automatically curving into the warm, familiar form next to her. Hans pulled her close with one arm, anchoring her against him.

## CHAPTER EIGHT

Envelopes sat on the table two days later when they arrived from the job site. Today, Hans and Gretel had alternated intensive jobs with less demanding ones to avoid being totally wiped out like usual. Hans stared at the white paper with his name on it and swallowed hard. He didn't expect any bad news from the testing but still it was ominous.

"Who goes first?" he asked. He knew that his results and Gretel's should be the exact same. He hadn't been with anyone since finding Gretel. There was no way she'd cheated on him, either. They were always together.

"I will go first. I have been tested recently and expect no problems. It's important that *you* know I want to protect you from everything I can," Magnus told them as he waved everyone into chairs.

Once seated, he carefully opened the envelope and pulled out the paper. Without delaying, Magnus smoothed the wrinkles from the sheet and turned it so they could read it with him. Hans looked at the result column. Negative, negative, negative... next to each test, that same word repeated.

Without speaking, Hans picked his up as well and tore it open. He peeked at the results and relaxed. He didn't expect anything bad to show up on his, but it was a relief to see it in black and white. Hans placed his results next to Magnus's.

"Open mine for me, Hans," Gretel requested in a tight voice that clued Hans in that she was stressed.

Magnus leaned over and picked Gretel up from her chair and held her in his lap, rocking her slightly. Hans tried to ignore the jealousy that flared inside him at the sight of them together. He tried to concentrate on how happy he was to see Gretel having time with their Daddy, but it was hard. He wanted the special attention.

"Thank you for opening it, sweet boy," Magnus said.

Shrugging away his thoughts, Hans tore open the envelope and found the sheet totally blank. There were no results on it. He turned around the paper and searched both their faces. "There's nothing here."

"What? There has to be results. I went. How else could they have my name?" Gretel protested.

"There were two envelopes with your name on it. I figured they were a duplicate and threw the other in the trash," Magnus shared.

Immediately, Gretel jumped to her feet and dashed to the trashcan. Finding a bunch of junk mail on the top, she snatched the duplicate envelope up and ripped it open, inadvertently tearing it in half. "Crap!"

"Bring it here, little girl," Magnus said, trying to hide his smile as Gretel pulled the two sides from the packaging and tried to match them in the air.

"There are words on here. Negative... negative... it's all negative," she crowed, dancing around.

"You goof," Hans stated, laughing, as he stood up to loop

his arms around Gretel's waist. He whirled her in a circle as she giggled.

When he'd set her back on her feet, Hans planted a kiss on her lips before she asked, "Why do we get all weirded out about these tests? We knew what they were going to say."

"It's important. Now we know beyond a shadow of a doubt that everyone is healthy and able to commit fully to a relationship," Hans told her and felt Magnus's large hand as the dynamic man stroked his back.

"That's it exactly. Now, how should we celebrate? Do you have enough energy to go to your favorite restaurant?" Magnus asked.

"We'll have to clean up first," Gretel said quickly.

Hans laughed as she tore off her shirt and ran for the shower. Yipping with delight, he followed her, undressing as he dashed down the hall. By the time he got to the bathroom, Gretel had stepped out of her jeans and panties. Her bra already lay abandoned on the floor. He devoured the sexy picture she made as Gretel leaned in to turn on the water. Clenching his teeth, Hans struggled to resist her allure.

"Maybe I should wait and take a shower after you," Hans suggested, pausing as his fingers latched inside the waistband of his pants.

"Get naked, little boy. We're not in any hurry. Dinner can wait if you can," Magnus suggested as he tugged his shirt off.

"You're showering with us?" Hans asked.

"Forever and ever," Magnus promised, stalking forward to force Hans backward toward the wall. He caged Hans against the hard surface and encircled his neck with one large hand, pressing him firmly against the cool wall paint. "You're mine now, little boy."

"Yours," Hans gasped and reached forward to draw Magnus toward him. His handsome Daddy moved forward quickly to capture Hans's lips and kiss him deeply. A quick gasp of breath made them both look to the side to see Gretel peeking around the shower wall.

"Don't mind me all wet and naked in here. You two just have fun out there," she teased.

Magnus looked at Hans and exchanged an undeniable message back and forth. As one, they separated and turned to stalk toward her, stepping out of their clothing as they moved.

"Eep!" Gretel squeaked and ducked back into the shower.

The two men bracketed her between them. Three pairs of hands touched and tempted each other as they exchanged kisses and caresses. Hans enjoyed watching everything. The sight of Magnus wet and fully aroused, pushed his excitement even higher. Add in their Daddy sharing his attention evenly between he and Gretel and Hans struggled for control.

As if understanding that the playtime in the shower challenged him, Magnus pumped liquid soap into his hands and smoothed it over Hans's body. Efficiently washing the day's labor from his skin, Magnus seemed to temper his caresses from pushing Hans over the edge as he kept Gretel on a high level of excitement. When they were both clean and rinsed, Magnus urged them out of the shower and dried their skin quickly before attending to himself.

"Bed, little ones," Magnus ordered, guiding them both into the bedroom. "I need you here for our first time together."

Both Littles paused at the foot of the bed. Hans reached out to squeeze Gretel's hand. He didn't know how Magnus would approach making love to them both. How would he balance their needs for his attention? Hans wanted Gretel to know that he was okay if their Daddy focused on her first. To his surprise, she pulled him forward to sit on the edge of the bed.

"I want to watch," she suggested.

Magnus had other ideas. "Lie back, Hans."

Not quite understanding what was going to happen, Hans rolled slowly onto his back. He stiffened as Magnus braced his hands on Hans's thighs and lowered himself to kneel in front of him. Using his hold, Magnus pressed those muscular thighs apart, drawing a low groan of anticipation from Hans.

"Gretel, I think Hans needs something to cover his eyes. Could you help him with that?" Magnus suggested.

When she started to place her hands over his eyelids, Hans caught on. "Straddle me, sweetpea."

"Oh!" Eagerly, Gretel moved into position. She allowed Hans to guide her down into position over his mouth and rocked against his caressing mouth. "Yes!"

Unable to see past the delectable treat above him, Hans felt her pause and knew something was coming. She had a ringside seat to watch Magnus's plans. As the hot mouth engulfed him, Hans struggled not to drive his hips forward and failed. Those powerful hands gripping his thighs restrained him, letting Hans know he wasn't in charge.

All possible thoughts other than pure enjoyment evaporated from his mind. The familiar, delicious treat that hovered over his lips enticed him to devour her sweetness as Magnus explored and teased his cock and balls. A tug to his tightening sac drew a groan from Hans's lips that sparked a "mmm" of enjoyment as the hum vibrated through Gretel's body as well. He loved the connection between them.

Soon, the skillful caresses proved too much for Hans. As he felt his orgasm approaching, he increased his attention to Gretel, wanting to take her with him. The high, keening sound that fell from her lips a few seconds later allowed him to relax his efforts to hold off the climax that tantalized him. With a shout into the room, Hans emptied himself into the wet heat that surrounded him.

Always wishing to take care of Gretel, he helped her shift

to lie next to him before reaching one arm out to Magnus. His Daddy immediately rose to lean over the bed to hold them. Hans ran a hand over Magnus' torso, tracing the grooves in his hard muscles. "Daddy, it's your turn. Let us please you."

"I get Daddy's attention now," Gretel demanded and leaned over to kiss Hans hard. "You always make me feel good," she whispered.

"I know, Gretel. It's your turn," Hans answered, amazed he did not feel jealous at all. He wanted to see Gretel with their Daddy.

With no awkwardness, Magnus shifted to kneel between Gretel's thighs. His hands explored Gretel's body, lingering here and there with special touches. "Help me, Hans. Show me what she likes most."

Instantly, Hans leaned forward to nibble the sensitive cord of her neck as his hand cupped and gently kneaded one breast. Magnus pressed kisses around the other before tasting Gretel's nipple.

"She likes it if you suck hard," Hans suggested, and watched as Magnus pulled the taut peak firmly into his mouth.

Gretel squeaked and wiggled beneath them. Her hips lifted to rub against the older man's hard stomach. Restraining her to the mattress as he had Hans, Magnus lifted his mouth from her and turned to cup Hans's skull, bringing his face close. He tasted Hans's lips, savoring the sweetness of the Little girl's juices that remained on his skin.

"Mmm. You are both delicious," he complimented before turning his attention back to Gretel.

Magnus stroked a hand over her body, drawing a trail of caresses to her core. "Do you need Daddy to wear a condom, sweetness?" he asked, brushing his fingers through her pink folds.

Hans watched Gretel struggle to understand the question. "She's protected by a birth control pill," he answered for her.

"Good girl," Magnus praised her.

"Please, Daddy. I need to feel you inside," she begged as she caressed both men.

Answering that plea, Magnus fitted himself against her and pushed forward as Hans tried to memorize the sight of his thick cock sliding inside. The image of taking Magnus into his own body flashed into his mind, and Hans felt his body respond eagerly. He traced his hands over their bodies, trying to pleasure them.

Gretel tilted her head back as her body stretched to allow Magnus to enter freely. The intense sensations played over her face as she enjoyed every inch of his generous shaft. Her hands clutched both his and Magnus's arms, drawing on their strength and support.

When his body met hers fully, Magnus leaned forward to kiss Gretel before exchanging a hard kiss with Hans. Moving within her, Magnus continued to weave his caresses between the two of them. His hand wrapped several times around Hans before Magnus drew Hans's hand to his own cock.

"Join us," he commanded as he sped up his thrusts into Gretel's responsive body.

His self-consciousness evaporated in the intimacy of their bedroom. He could be himself here. Pulling on his cock, he felt it lengthen to full size as Gretel's eyes focused on him. Distracted by her attention, he gasped when Magnus wrapped a hand around his to caress his shaft as well.

Hans lost himself in the exchange of exquisite caresses and steaming kisses. Their bodies moved together easily, as if they'd done this a million times before, but with the excitement of discovering new ways to please each other.

When they lay in an exhausted pile together on the bed,

Hans clung to the two people he cherished most in the world. "Daddy," he breathed out as he squeezed Gretel's hand.

"We could have missed this," Gretel said in awe of the series of events that had brought them together.

"Littles never can resist sweets. My gingerbread house was destined to find you," Magnus assured them. "Now I plan to keep you."

"Yessss," Hans sighed, drawing out that last consonant.

## CHAPTER NINE

The days blended together as the house seemed to stand taller and prouder on the beautiful lot. Gretel loved all the small touches Hans added outside to make the home special. She worked just as hard on the interior. The combination of all the inside and outside improvements started to make the old, battered Victorian feel revived and alive once again. She loved how it seemed to welcome her every day with a bit more enthusiasm.

When a sudden idea burst into her mind, Gretel ran out the front door to find him. Racing around the back of the house, she discovered him adding embellishments to the deck supports.

"Hans! I have an idea. You know how Daddy loves the sauna at the gym? What do you think about building one in at the back of the house for him?" she proposed.

"We'd have to run it by him first as an overage," Hans answered slowly as he considered it.

"Not if it's a gift to Daddy from us. Like a housewarming present."

"Like a real house 'warming' present?" Hans laughed. "That's an amazing idea. He'd share it with us, too. I could use a sauna to loosen up my muscles."

"Is it too late to add the wiring that a sauna would require? We could just buy one and set it on the concrete by the back door," she suggested.

"Hell, no. If we're going to have a sauna, I'm going to build him something special." Hans ran a hand over his head as he thought. "It'll take a few days. Think we can keep him from going behind the house?"

"He always walks around it," Gretel reminded him. "We'd have to tell him we're adding something in the back and ask that he let it be a surprise."

"You're right. Hopefully, he'll trust us enough to stay away," Hans said, distractedly.

She could tell he was already making mental plans and shopping lists. Gretel smiled broadly when he walked toward the area she'd been considering the perfect spot, muttering to himself. Hans would make this the shining star of all saunas for their Daddy. Hugging herself with excitement, Gretel headed inside to work on the thousand small details that remained for her to attack.

Time passed quickly as she installed light fixtures and added trim around built-in furniture. She sent a kiss message to Magnus and then asked if he'd be available to ask about furniture for the house. Gretel shook her head, not believing they hadn't taken time to discuss such an important matter. She was sure she'd returned to her Daddy's house with that thought in mind several times. Somehow, he always distracted her.

"I'd love to talk to you, sweetness," Magnus' voice boomed from the doorway, making her jump seconds later.

"Daddy!"

Leaping to her feet, she ran to jump into his arms. "Hi!"

"Hi!" Magnus returned her excited greeting with the same happiness to see her woven in. He drew her face to hers and kissed her lightly before setting her firmly away. "You, minx, have distracted us from chatting about that exact thing for days."

"No! It was you!" She laughed, delighted he had lost track of important tasks as well.

"We're both here and there's too many workers around for us to check out the bedroom. Shall we talk now?"

Giggling, she nodded. "Let's talk."

Gretel grabbed a pad of paper. "We'll walk through the house and I'll take notes. We're here in the family room. I can definitely see the leather sectional arranged here with a big television..." She paused for a second and wondered if she should say something.

"What are you thinking, sweetness?" Magnus probed.

"I don't want to assume anything."

"I'm not following you, little girl."

"Do you want Hans and me to live with you when the house is finished? Is that your plan?" she blurted.

"Of course. I just found you. It would tear my heart out if you left me when the house was finished. Why is this coming up, little girl? Do you and Hans have second thoughts about our relationship?"

The concern that etched itself into his brow hurt Gretel's heart. She quickly shook her head to deny that idea. "Oh, no. We love being with you. I-I love you, Daddy." She rushed forward to throw herself into his arms and clung to his hard body.

"Hey! I saw your car and came to say hello... is something going on?" Hans asked as he looked at Gretel plastered to Magnus.

"I think I misunderstood what Gretel said," Magnus suggested.

Lifting her tear-stained face, Gretel said in a voice rocked with emotion, "I didn't mean anything bad. I was talking about the room and thought the TV from our place would be better here in the new family room. Then I got scared that maybe... Magnus wouldn't want us here when we got everything finished."

"I love you, too, little girl," Magnus shared tenderly and kissed her before holding a hand out to Hans and pulling him close. "I love you, little boy. I don't plan on ever letting you go."

"I love you, Daddy," Hans said and wrapped his arms around them.

The trio stood united in the quiet of the room, with echoes of construction surrounding their small, intimate bubble. Gretel's tears evaporated as the warmth from the men burned away the chill that had settled around her heart.

"I caused so much trouble," she whispered.

"No, you did not. This is entirely my fault. I assumed you both understood that this would be our home and didn't discuss my plans directly with you both. Assuming is never a good idea, and I apologize for not making this clear for you."

Magnus focused back on Gretel before adding, "When we're alone, or even if you choose when we're with others, it's Daddy, not Magnus."

"Yes, Daddy."

"And I want to make sure you know I am not in a relationship with you two because I think that will help me with the house remodel, little girl," Magnus said sternly, looking between the two Littles. "This house means nothing without you now. You two have made it a home."

"I just didn't want to sound pushy or expect something that we hadn't talked about," Gretel protested. Her lips curved into a tremulous smile at his words and she tried to get ahold of herself, scrubbing the tears from her face.

"You're the sweetness in our relationship. You could never be pushy," Magnus assured her.

"Should we talk now?" Hans asked.

"We should make plans now. Let's go from room to room together. Gretel can give us her idea of what would be best in the room and then we see if we have it in either of our temporary places or if we need to go on a shopping spree. Before you worry about that, I can afford everything but gold-crusted swans in the bathroom."

The two Littles giggled at that idea. "On my list. No gilded waterfowl," Gretel jotted down at the top of the page.

They worked their way methodically through the house. It turned out that they had some special pieces they'd gathered from other properties or salvaged from owners who discarded them. Once restored to their former brilliance by the Littles' skills, the items looked spectacular. Gretel was especially thrilled to have the perfect spot for a set of floor to ceiling bookshelves, featuring a gliding ladder to climb to get items at the top.

When she showed Magnus a picture of the restoration, he picked her up and twirled her in a circle. "That's incredible. I'll get a special sticker for anything you bring in to mark that it's yours. I don't ever plan to let you go, but if something happens and you decide to leave, I want to make sure your property is clearly yours."

"We're not going to leave," Hans stated emphatically.

"Nope," Gretel answered.

Sensing Magnus was suggesting something might happen to him, Gretel forced herself to change the subject. "There's only one floor left. Shall we head to the basement?"

"I have a suggestion for the basement," Magnus teased.

"Really? Well, let's go," Hans said, waving a hand toward the stairway.

At the bottom of the stairs, Hans flipped on the lights and illuminated a space completely different from the dark, scary place they'd first walked into. Hans had supervised the restoration of the stained and pitted foundation. He'd ensured it was solid and strong enough to last another hundred years, at least. Now, the area featured white walls, modern lighting and durable flooring. The only remanent left was the iron cage which had taken Hans the good part of a day to brush away the surface rust and give a protective coating.

"What do you want to do with this, Daddy?" Hans asked, wrapping his fingers around a metal bar.

"I think we need a play room down here. Who knows if we might have a kitty, doggie, or naughty Little who needs a time out?" Magnus suggested.

"You could put Hans in there when he doesn't eat his dinner," Gretel suggested, referring to the previous evening when Hans had spent time in the corner with a red bottom for refusing to eat two bites of the spinach casserole.

"I hate that two-bite rule. Who wants to take a second bite of something they already know is horrible?" Hans muttered.

"You enjoyed it in this morning's omelet," Magnus suggested.

"That was spinach dip... like you get at Mexican restaurants. It's not really spinach," Hans pointed out. "It's more cheese."

"It was exactly the same thing. You would have liked it last night but you wouldn't try it. It was my suggestion to make the omelet this morning. I knew you'd tried those before and would at least take a taste," she said quickly, before Hans accused Magnus of trying to trick him.

"That's not fair. You ganged up on me. I'm never going to trust you again," Hans lashed out.

"I think it's time for you to get in the cage, Hans," Magnus said quietly.

"So, I get punished again when people lied to me?"

"I think you need a quiet place to think before you say mean things to Gretel."

Even though he already regretted speaking harshly to Gretel and making her look so sad, Hans was mad. With a huff, he slammed open the door and crawled in, closing himself inside. Dramatically, he announced, "I'll just never say anything at all." Pantomiming locking his lips closed, he tossed the imaginary key away.

Magnus and Gretel sat down next to the cage and continued to design the space. They added a changing station and a big comfortable couch with the latest gaming system and a huge TV. Turning their attention to the space around the cage, Gretel requested walls around one section of the large space.

"When I'm in this… kinky area, I want to be protected. To know that only you and Hans know what I'm feeling and needing," she explained.

"I'm sure Hans can make that happen easily. I bet he'd prefer that, too. Instead of seeing even small windows looking out into the backyard when he's restrained, he'd most likely prefer to know that only you and I are there to see his reactions," Magnus suggested.

Gretel looked over at Hans, who had settled with his back against the bars as close to her and their Daddy as possible. She saw him nod and said, "I think you're right. That makes more sense."

She hesitated for a minute, debating how to ask for something. Finally, Gretel just allowed the words to rush from her mouth. "Can we have a spanking bench?"

"Definitely. And an examination table. I need to make sure that you are healthy," Magnus added.

Gretel saw Hans shiver inside the cage and knew that was a fantasy of his. "We'd need to store supplies, I guess?"

"I could make a false wall over there that hides stuff," Hans whispered with a wave of his hand.

"That would be incredible, little boy. Could it be big enough to have hooks and shelves?" Magnus asked without reacting to Hans dropping out of his self-enforced silence.

"Yes. That would be easy if Gretel draws it out for me," Hans suggested with a meaningful look at her.

"I'll do it tonight when we get home," she promised.

Magnus gently prodded Hans through the cage bars. "You seem to be better. When you're upset, your whole body gets rigid. You feel more relaxed now. Are you ready to come out and talk to us?"

"Yes, please," Hans said quietly. He waited for Magnus to open the unlocked cage and then crawled out. "I'm sorry I was awful. Was that goop really the cheesy stuff in the eggs this morning?"

"It was," Magnus confirmed.

"And I could have found that out if I'd only followed your two-bite rule?"

"Definitely."

"I'm an absolute idiot!" Hans exclaimed. "I'm sorry for talking meanly to you." He dropped his head down as he looked at the floor they all sat on.

Gretel reached over and patted his knee. "It's okay. Everyone gets to have an off day." When he smiled at her kindness, she warned, "Just don't have one of those yucky days constantly."

"Your bottom will get very sore," Magnus suggested.

"Are you going to spank me?" Hans asked with horror in his eyes.

"No. I'm going to increase the size of the plug in your bottom two steps tonight," Magnus told him nonchalantly. To prepare the Littles to take him without pain, their Daddy plugged both Hans and Gretel's bottoms, increasing the size each week.

"Two steps?" Hans echoed.

"Me, too?" Gretel asked with a quavering voice.

"I'll let Hans decide that. Does he still think you should be punished for lying to him?" Magnus asked, looking back and forth between the duo.

Gretel bit her bottom lip. How mad was Hans?

After a brief pause, Hans shook his head. "No. She was trying to help me."

"I think we've done enough planning tonight. Let's go home," Magnus suggested.

Hans nodded as if he were going to his fate. Gretel crossed her fingers. Her Daddy could work miracles. Could he make this lesson have a positive side as well?

## CHAPTER
# TEN

Hans knew he parked a bit wonky in the driveway that night. Gretel had ridden home with him and chattered the whole way to try to distract him. It hadn't worked.

He walked into the house slowly, trying to drag it out, and ran to the bathroom to give himself a minute. When he came out of the toilet area, Magnus leaned against the vanity.

"Are you okay, Hans?" his Daddy asked.

"Yes. I'm really sorry," he repeated.

"I know you are. Come on. Gretel's waiting for you."

He steered Hans down the hallway to the brightly lit kitchen. Hans swallowed hard at the sight of Gretel lying over the kitchen table, her jeans and panties removed. Staring at her small, rounded bottom, Hans felt bad that he'd made her wait.

"Let's get you ready," his Daddy suggested. He guided Hans to face him and quickly unfastened his jeans and pushed them and his boxer briefs to the floor.

Hans breathed a sigh of relief that he wasn't smelly or covered with building materials. He wouldn't knock Magnus over with his outdoor laborer scent. Dragging his thoughts away from his worries, he focused on his Daddy's next directions.

"Step out of your things and take them to the laundry room."

When Hans returned, he watched Gretel scoop her clothes off the floor and head for the laundry room. Not waiting for her, Hans quickly leaned over the table and waited for Gretel to join him. He whispered, "Sorry" and the sweet woman reached out her hand to take his. Hans squeezed her fingers.

"Gretel's first tonight," their Daddy reminded them as he unzipped the large black case containing two sets of matched metal plugs in a variety of thicknesses. He set it down where they could both see it and selected two plugs. The size Hans and Gretel were supposed to wear for the next three days and the one two steps larger. He set each one on the table.

Hans gritted his teeth. *One hundred. Ninety-nine. Ninety-eight...* he tried to count backward in his brain to distract himself from the thought of that huge invader going inside him. It wasn't working. He shifted on the table to allow his stiffening penis to adjust.

With a click, Hans heard the lid of the lubricant open. He felt Gretel shift on the table and knew that their Daddy had spread her bottom to reveal the small opening hidden there. His hand plucked the device from the table and Gretel bit her bottom lip as he slowly inserted it fully. Her eyes closed and Hans knew their Daddy was adjusting it by moving the plug in and out until Gretel relaxed. Soon, her body softened. The sound of the familiar pat on her bare bottom followed, letting her know she'd done a good job. Their Daddy always reassured them.

"Hans's turn," his Daddy announced.

He seemed to move in slow motion as Magnus parted his

bottom. The lubricant dripped slowly onto his clenched ring of muscles, and Hans saw him reach for the plug. The first touch always felt so cold. He shivered on the table and Gretel squeezed his hand.

The plug didn't seem so bad as it slid inside until the thick part stretched him. Magnus never rushed or slowed down. He pressed the device steadily into place as Hans attempted to wiggle, but Magnus' powerful hand over his tailbone held him in place. He could feel it press directly against a super zingy spot inside him. Finally, it was in.

He slumped on the table only to rear his head up as his Daddy pulled it back out and started the process again. "It was good," he protested.

"Daddy's in charge, little boy. It needs to be better than good. It needs to be perfect. Scoot back a bit and boost your hips up. This larger plug needs more space," Magnus suggested.

As Hans moved, Magnus lifted the hand, restraining him to the table to help him adjust. Hans breathed a sigh of relief as the pressure eased on his erection. His teeth clacked together when that powerful hand wrapped around his shaft and squeezed just as his Daddy applied the plug again. It took three tries for Magnus to be satisfied by the placement of the thick device. Hans sweated as he tried to stop himself from exploding.

"Good job, little boy. Good job, Gretel. You can sit at your spot at the table and I'll dish up dinner."

Pushing himself up from the table, Hans sat on the towel placed on his chair to keep the lubricant from staining the fabric. "Two hours?" he asked his Daddy. That was usually all they had to wear the plug.

"Two hours, little boy." Magnus reassured him with a kiss before moving to wash his hands.

It felt so naughty sitting half naked at the table. Thank goodness the table in front of him covered his erection. Each time he shifted, that plug in his bottom moved against his most sensitive spots. All he could think of was sex with Magnus. He was on a hair trigger. Hans pulled down the T-shirt he'd worn to work that still covered his upper half. Hans looked over at Gretel when he felt her sock-covered foot brush over his calf.

"Are you okay?" she mouthed.

Hans leaned forward to whisper. "I may die."

"Does it hurt?"

He paused and admitted, "No. It feels way too good."

"Oh! That is a problem."

"Don't laugh," Hans demanded, feeling so vulnerable.

"I wouldn't laugh at you. Let's change the subject. Did you talk to Daddy about the—"

"About what?" Magnus asked, placing a large serving dish on the table between them.

"Maybe this isn't the best time," Hans suggested as his Daddy ladled a delicious smelling mixture of vegetables and shrimp onto his plate before adding a spoonful of rice in the middle.

"This is a perfect time. What's up?"

"The job is wrapping up soon and we want to do something special for you," Gretel explained as her Daddy served her as well.

"I think you've both done a lot for me already," Magnus answered and filled his own plate.

"No. This is something different. Hans and I want to do something special for our Daddy in our new home," Gretel explained.

"Tell me more."

"That's just it! We can't. It would ruin the surprise," Hans said quickly.

"A surprise, hmm?"

"Yes, Daddy. Could you help us by not going out into the backyard?" Gretel asked.

Magnus looked back and forth between his Littles with a thoughtful expression. "I can't think of anyone else I'd trust more. I'll make you a deal. I'll stay out of the backyard and you both stay away from the nursery."

"That room off the main bedroom?" Gretel asked.

"That's the one," he answered with a smile.

"Deal!" Hans agreed immediately.

"Wait! What's happening in the nursery?" Gretel asked curiously.

"What's happening in the backyard?" Magnus flipped around the question.

"Deal," Gretel agreed reluctantly, after thinking about it for a few seconds.

Hans knew her curiosity about the room was going to be a problem. He quickly changed the subject to discuss the progress they'd made that day in the house. Magnus was always excited to hear even the smallest improvement and Gretel always had something to ask her Daddy's opinion on. They chattered happily for the rest of the meal.

He knew he was quieter than usual but couldn't do anything about that. The plug was driving him crazy, no matter how Hans tried to distract himself. Even the smallest movement jostled the large object inside him.

As normal after finishing the meal, they had to sit quietly as Magnus cleaned up the kitchen and made their lunches for the next day. Hans folded his hands on top of the table to keep from touching himself. His desire had skyrocketed throughout the meal. His Daddy's innocent touches had felt like lightning bolts on his skin that connected directly to his cock.

When Magnus folded the kitchen towel and placed it neatly on the rack, Hans knew he was finished in the kitchen. Legs wobbly, Hans stood up without being asked and laid flat against the tabletop to have the plug removed. When his Daddy smoothed a hand down his spine to cup one buttock, Hans held his breath.

"You did a good job taking this plug, little boy. I think you might be ready for me to make love to you," Magnus suggested.

"Really?" Hans peeked over his shoulder to look at the large man behind him. He glanced at Gretel to make sure she was okay. Her hands were clasped between her breasts and she vibrated with excitement. "But what about Gretel?"

"There will be times that I have special time with each of you alone, but this is a time for us together."

Magnus waited for each of them to nod their agreement. Then he carefully removed their plugs and ushered them from the kitchen. As they passed through the doorway into the hall, Magnus pulled Hans close for a kiss before sharing one with Gretel. She looped her arms around Hans's neck and rubbed her face under his jaw, planting sweet kisses on a path to the neck of his T-shirt.

Jumping back, she yanked the hem of her T-shirt over her head and dropped it on the carpet before demanding Hans take his off, too. "You don't need this!"

Hans cooperated eagerly and dropped his shirt a few steps further down the hall. Their socks soon littered the carpet as well. As they stepped into the bedroom, Hans nodded at Gretel and knew she understood. It was their Daddy's turn.

"Hold it right there, littles. Daddy's in charge. Go sit on the edge of the bed."

Taking Gretel's hand, Hans led her to the king-size bed and perched on the edge. She squeezed his hand as Magnus pulled his shirt over his head and worked on removing his jeans. With each handsome inch of their mesmerizing Daddy coming into view, Hans got a bit more nervous. What if he didn't please his Daddy?

"Stop it," Gretel hissed, obviously sensing the tension in his body.

"I can't," Hans whispered back.

"Gretel, I think Hans is too tense. Would you like to help him relax a bit?" Magnus asked. He paused in undressing himself, leaving his fly open and his erection straining at his snug boxer briefs.

"I would love to help," Gretel said, instantly.

"Kneel in front of Hans and take him into your mouth. He'll return the favor soon," Magnus promised.

Eagerly, Gretel slid to the floor and scooted in front of Hans. Familiar with his body, she wrapped her hand around his erection. Hans fought not to buck his hips up off the bed or lose control.

"I can feel you pulsing in my hand," Gretel whispered to him. She squeezed experimentally, and Hans bit his lip, strangling his moan.

"What would happen if I…" Allowing that question to linger in the air, she leaned forward to lick the broad head of his cock.

That was all it took. Gretel sealed her lips around him as Hans lost control. He gripped the comforter under him for stability as she milked his fluid from his shaft. Panting in reaction, Hans could only look at the man who watched. To his delight, Magnus stroked his erection, pulling roughly.

"I'll have to remember that size plug had such a reaction,

little boy. Do you think you should taste Gretel now?" Magnus asked.

"Yes, Daddy."

"Gretel, crawl onto the bed and put your head on the covers." He waited until she was settled. "Hans, taste Gretel. Leave your bottom up in the air for Daddy,"

"Up for Daddy?" Hans repeated, feeling his body rallying to respond. He moved slowly, trying to do the right thing and looking back frequently.

Kissing a line down the center of Gretel's body, he paused over her small mound. "Thank you, Gretel, for helping me come. Let me help you now."

"Please!" she said, nodding eagerly.

He stroked his tongue through her pink folds. Her familiar scent and taste filled his senses. Gretel loved having him pleasure her this way and Hans couldn't get enough of watching her explode. She was already wiggling underneath him when Hans felt Magnus's hands stroke over his buttocks.

"Spread your knees, Hans. Daddy wants to settle right here between them."

The feel of Magnus's lightly furred thighs pressing his apart made Hans almost forget Gretel below him. He quickly made it up to her by circling her clit with his tongue and sucking lightly. Her fingers tangled in his hair and pulled slightly to thank him.

The snap of the lubricant brought his head up. He started to look over his shoulder, but Gretel held him steady. "Daddy's taking care of you, Hans."

He nodded and moaned against her as Magnus's thick fingers pressed into him, spreading the slick lubricant thoroughly. Hans mirrored the action and slid two fingers into Gretel's tight channel. He lowered his hips slightly to grind his cock against the comforter.

"Uh, uh, little boy," Magnus warned him, as he wrapped his free arm around Hans's waist to tug his bottom back into position. "Daddy wants you right here."

"His cock is huge," Gretel warned, watching the show over Hans's back.

"That doesn't help, Gretel," Hans hissed against her body, making her wiggle from the vibrations of his voice.

When the fingers left their explorations inside Hans, he knew what was coming next. Torn between excitement and the fear of the unknown, he focused on Gretel. She was his best friend. *And she's watching.* That thought made him tremble with arousal and apprehension.

Magnus's hand smoothed over his butt. "Such a good Little boy. You deserve Daddy's attention, don't you?"

"Please," Hans begged.

Immediately, the man behind him pressed the broad head of his cock against Hans. He pushed relentlessly, sliding his thick cock into Hans—slowly and deliberately filling his tight channel. Hans lifted his head as the sensations overwhelmed him. Magnus ground the thick base of his shaft against Hans's sensitive entrance.

"You feel so good, Hans. Daddy's going to want to play inside you often. Would you like that, Hans?"

"Please."

A warm hand wrapped around Hans's cock and pulled as Magnus withdrew from him. And reversed the process as he thrust back in, faster this time. Pleasure overwhelmed Hans at the hint of pain from the stretch of the thick shaft filling him and sensitive spots inside his body that Magnus lavished attention on each time he filled him.

Hans saw Gretel's hands move between her legs as she pleasured herself. The view of her masturbating to the scene playing out over her further stimulated Hans. Sorry that he had forgotten to include her, Hans slid one hand under her small bottom and lifted her to his mouth, adding to the sensations she lavished on herself.

Unable to focus on any one thing, Hans simply allowed himself to feel. Gretel cried out as she climaxed. Her body trembled below him delectably. A slap to his bottom made Hans lose control, and he shouted his climax into the room. His body locking around Magnus sparked his Daddy's climax.

"Mine!" Magnus uttered, claiming them both.

Soon, the two men lie on either side of Gretel, cuddling her between them. Magnus kissed her softly before leaning over to kiss Hans, as well. "I can't imagine my life without the two of you in it. Hans, you were delectable and so brave. I'm very proud of you and can't wait to bury myself in your bottom again."

Hans felt his skin heat and knew he was blushing. He squeezed his bottom, feeling the soreness that triggered his memories of taking his Daddy inside. "I can't wait either, Daddy," he admitted.

"Next time, it will be Gretel's turn to be the center of our sandwich," Magnus declared. "She'll have to wear the big plug soon to take both of us."

Hans felt Gretel shiver and noted that she wasn't scared but aroused. He knew their adventures together would be even more satisfying with their Daddy. A huge yawn widened his mouth, surprising him. He settled a bit closer to Gretel and closed his eyes. A soft cover settled over him, making him smile. His Daddy was taking care of him.

# CHAPTER
# ELEVEN

Gretel stepped into the gorgeous red wood sauna. It was simple but included all the perfect touches that she knew their Daddy would love. She added a hook and hung a heart she'd created out of the scraps of the cedar left over from the building project. Meticulously, she'd carved each of their names separated by interlocking hearts with Magnus in the middle. It added the final touch to make it theirs.

"When are we going to show it to him?" Hans asked.

"Oh! You scared me. Shall we show him tonight when the workers are gone?" she asked, feeling her heart rate settle.

"I can't wait to see the nursery. I've been so tempted to go look at it when Magnus is away but I couldn't. He's been so good about not trying to see ours."

"I know. It's tearing me apart. Let's show him tonight and hope he shows us, too."

"Smart. Let's do it." Hans pulled out his phone and texted his Daddy, asking if he could come to the site around six that night.

Gretel grinned when her phone rang as well. She loved their group text. It kept each of the Littles from feeling that there was some kind of secret communication. She didn't want to feel jealous and Magnus did everything he could do to include them both.

"He's going to be here at six," she reported.

"Good. Hey. There's a second message. Magnus wants to pick you up at ten for coffee. Just you and him," Hans reported, meeting Gretel's gaze. "I'm supposed to tell you."

"That's weird." She almost dropped her phone when it buzzed with an incoming message. Looking down, she read, *Tell Hans.*

"I'm supposed to tell you that Daddy's coming to take you for malts at two."

"Just me and Daddy?" he asked.

"I guess."

"He's making a date with each of us separately but making sure we both know it. That's fun. We'll each have some individual Daddy time. You've only got six minutes."

"Crap. My hair!"

~

As she went tearing out to run to the house, Hans followed at a more sedate pace. He circled the house to wait for Magnus. Exactly on time, the handsome man pulled up in his car.

"Hans! I'm glad I got to see you this morning," Magnus said as he got out of the car. He stalked forward to wrap his arms around Hans and pulled him close to hug and kiss.

Hans had felt funny in the beginning of being open about their relationship in front of their crews who were working. Magnus had not allowed him to hide. He didn't expose Hans's secret Little side but taught him that people really didn't care who you loved.

"I like this idea of having some alone time with you," Hans admitted.

"It's important for me to get to spoil each of you individually. We'll see how this does and if you think it's important to continue. I do, but I want to hear your opinion, too."

"Hi, Daddy!"

The men turned to see Gretel with her hair neatly combed and lip gloss applied. She looked adorable to Hans. Throwing her arms around Magnus first, she kissed him lightly before treating Hans to a hug and kiss as well.

"Hi, Gretel. Are you ready for a coffee break?" Magnus asked.

"I'm so ready."

Turning to Hans, she double checked, "You're okay if I go with Magnus?"

"I'll have my time this afternoon. Go have fun."

He watched Magnus help Gretel into the car before he forced himself to turn and head back in the house. There were a million small details to take care of and he wanted the house in the best shape. He checked to make sure the decorative trim was dry. Called the gingerbread, the lacy pieces would fit around the edge of the porch to give the house an almost candy-like appeal.

Thrilled that it was ready to go, Hans carefully nailed it in place. It was easy work but had to be placed exactly correctly. He filled in the nail holes to ensure nothing detracted from the allure of the quaint decoration. He'd just finished and was moving the ladder out of the way when Magnus appeared.

He could see the delight on Gretel's face as they pulled up. Magnus had to shake his finger at her to remind her to wait for him to open the door for her. As he swung the car door open, she burst from the car. Racing to Hans's side, she threw her arms around him and bounced up and down.

"You got it up. It looks so incredible. How can that one thing make such a difference?"

"I thought you'd like this."

"Like it? I love it! It's like we get to live in a house made of candy. Like the storybook's Hansel and Gretel."

"I hope you're not going to throw me in a hot oven," Magnus said, laughing.

Hans and Gretel didn't look at each other. They hadn't even imagined that the story could have a parallel ending. "We'd never roast you alive, Daddy. That's a horrible thought," Hans said, trying not to give their secret away.

"I'm glad to hear that. Hans, be ready at two and save room for a malt."

"I will, Daddy."

The two Littles waved as he drove away. The minute he faded from sight, Hans asked, "Did you have fun?"

"I did. He took me to the coffee place and bought me a triple-chocolate latte. It was delicious!"

"That does sound good," Hans said with a grin. Magnus couldn't have chosen a better date with Gretel. She loved froufrou coffee drinks.

"Then we talked about all sorts of things—the house, my life, my dream vacation, and you."

"You talked about me during your alone time with Daddy?" Hans asked, astounded. "You didn't tell him all my faults, did you?"

"No. I told him how important you are to me and how much I love you," Gretel confessed.

Hans pulled her close and kissed her. "I love you, too. I'm so proud of us for being honest with each other that we both felt like we needed a Daddy."

"Me, too. I've always felt like I could tell you anything. Like..." Her voice trailed off, making Hans nervous.

"Like what?"

"You missed a section of the gingerbread."

"No way! Where?" He demanded, looking back at the porch. He watched Gretel walk up to a place where two porch supports met. Sure enough, there was a small gap there. Triumphantly, he pulled the piece from his pocket and waved it.

"Yes. I needed you. I had the piece but couldn't find where it goes. Don't move. Let me grab a hammer."

Within seconds, he had it fixed. After dropping the hammer in his tool belt, he pressed a light kiss on her lips. "Thanks, partner."

"Any time. Now it's perfect."

"Come find something else I've missed. I need to stay busy until two and my date with Daddy," Hans urged.

~

AT TEN MINUTES TO TWO, Hans stuck his head under the spigot to cool off and get some of the sweat off him. He carefully washed his hands and arms, trying to make himself presentable. Gretel had kept him busy as he'd requested. That made the time go fast, but he hadn't meant to get so sweaty.

A large hand cupped his butt. Hans swung around immediately and let out a breath of relief when he saw Magnus. "That scared me."

"I hope no one else pats your bottom," Magnus said, looking serious.

"No one. Well, maybe Gretel if she's goofing around. But no one else," Hans rushed to assure him.

"I'm glad." A smile transformed his face from serious to delighted.

Hans found himself grinning back at him. He loved spending time with his Daddy.

"Are you ready to go?" Magnus asked.

"I'm so sorry. I don't know if you even want to take me. I'm a sweaty mess," Hans confessed.

"We're not going anywhere fancy. I promised you a malt. Let's go get you somewhere cool."

"That sounds heavenly, Daddy."

Within a short time, Magnus found Gretel to tell her he was stealing Hans and to nab a kiss from her as well. He buckled Hans securely into the passenger seat and they waved goodbye to Gretel standing on the porch. She playfully pretended like she was gnawing on the fancy gingerbread.

"She's so much fun," Hans said when they were out of sight.

"Gretel loves with all her heart and lives life to the fullest. It's quite rare for a woman to have the skills she possesses. Your company is rare. To have two skilled craft people together on a job is amazing."

"I'm lucky I found her."

"And she feels the same way. I do as well. Look, there's the place."

"They have the best ice cream here," Hans said, leaning forward.

A car speeding through a red light made Magnus brake suddenly, and he threw out an arm automatically to keep Hans safe. "Whew. That was close." He patted Hans on the chest and continued on to turn into the shop.

Feeling his heart swell in his chest, Hans swallowed his emotions. What an amazing Daddy whose first thought was to make sure that he was okay. He followed Magnus in and they slid into a corner booth in the back. With his brain running in a thousand different directions, Hans couldn't decide what to order.

"Hi, guys. What can I get you?" a chipper waitress asked.

"I'd like a chocolate mint milkshake," Magnus ordered.

"What's the special?" Hans asked, hoping that it would sound good, so he didn't have to decide between all the others.

"It's a peach shake with real peach pieces," she offered.

"Done. I want that. A large, please. And a glass of water," Hans requested.

"Can I change my order?" Magnus jumped in before she could go put in their choices. "That sounds amazing."

"You won't regret it. They're delicious." Making a note on her pad, she headed to the front of the store.

"That was smart to ask for the special," Magnus complimented.

"I was having trouble focusing on the menu. I'm a bit wound up to be here with you," he confessed.

"I'm excited to be with you as well. Do you have anything you'd like to talk about?" Magnus asked.

"Could you tell me about yourself? I'd like to know more about you."

"Of course. Jump in and tell me things about you, too."

Magnus talked easily about his life and the things he loved. It was easy to relax and learn about his life prior to buying his home. By the time the peach milkshakes came, Hans had forgotten about being nervous and was having a great time. Having his Daddy to himself was fun, but he found himself trying to remember different things to tell Gretel.

*Slurrrp!!!* Hans sucked up the last bit of deliciousness out of the fancy glass. "That was delicious."

"The best milkshake I've ever had," Magnus agreed. "Ready to go back to see Gretel?"

"Yes, please. Daddy, I have to tell you something. I really enjoyed having you to myself today, but I kept thinking about how much learning about you would have thrilled Gretel as well."

Magnus leaned in and whispered confidentially, "Gretel said the exact same thing."

"No way! She didn't tell me that."

"Good. She wasn't supposed to. This wasn't a test, Hans. I wanted to give you each a chance to have all my attention. What you all taught me is how much you love each other. I needed to know that. Let's go back and find Gretel."

"Let's go!"

## CHAPTER TWELVE

When they got back to the house, Magnus shared the good news with Gretel. Hans could see the relief on her face, and he was so glad he'd listened to that voice in the back of his brain, telling him that something else would be even better.

"Can I see my surprise yet?" Magnus asked.

"It would be better if we waited until the workers head home in an hour. Do you have time to run through the house and see everything? I think we'll be ready to hand the keys back to you next week," Gretel suggested.

"I'm ready to be home. Let's go look at all you've accomplished," Magnus agreed.

Weaving their way around the guys finishing up the tiled entry and showers, Hans led the way through each room. They ended up on the top floor that had a bird's eye view of the surrounding property. Hans and Gretel stood blocking the window overlooking the back of the house.

Magnus jumped, trying out the solidity of the floor. "I'm not going through that."

"No way. This house will be here for another century. It was a lot of work, but we've renovated everything—plumbing, structure, wiring, heating and air conditioning. You have a brand-new house inside a charming and unique exterior," Hans told him.

"We have a brand-new house. You'll sleep with Daddy, of course. That leaves some bedrooms open. Would you like this one for your office?" Magnus offered.

"I don't want to work here. Hans and I will keep our office separate from our together time. When we're off a job, I don't want to think about it," Gretel admitted, and Hans immediately nodded his agreement.

"Then we'll do something else with this room. There's no need to decide today. I wouldn't mind having a library. The light up here is amazing. I could put shelves there and a desk for myself. Maybe a chaise lounge to stretch out on and read."

"That sounds wonderful. We can definitely add shelves up here," Hans chimed in.

"We'll hold off on any more home improvements until we get moved in and find out what the house offers and we need," Magnus suggested.

"That's a good idea," Gretel agreed.

Pointing to the front of the house, she said, "What good timing. That's the last truck to leave. It's time for us to show you our surprise."

Eagerly, they led Magnus to the main level and then out the back door. The last guys leaving had removed the temporary screens Hans had constructed to help them keep the secret. Walking out onto the deck first, Hans turned to watch his Daddy's face.

"That isn't… is that a sauna?" Magnus looked dumbfounded.

"It is. Want to try it out?" Gretel cheered.

"I'm going to live in there. Let's go." Magnus walked forward to open the door.

There was a small antechamber with benches. Thick towels hung on one wall, waiting for them. Hans showed Magnus the hidden panel of controls and turned it on. "We get undressed in here and then go inside to feel the heat."

"You made me an oven," Magnus laughed.

"We promise we won't shove you in and lock the door," Gretel teased as she stripped out of her clothes. "Watch this!" She stepped to one side and tapped a button. Cool water cascaded down from above as she rotated underneath it.

"That's a great idea. You can cool off before trying to get dressed," Magnus said, shaking his head in amazement. "You two thought of everything."

"You go in first, Daddy," Hans invited when everyone was naked.

Magnus led the way as the Littles trailed behind them.

"Whoa! What are you watching?" Hans said, laughing when Gretel plowed into the back of him. "Daddy stopped to look around. I stopped behind him and you just kept walking."

"I must have been thinking too hard," Gretel tried to excuse herself.

"I think you were watching Daddy's butt." Hans smirked.

"Hans, don't tease Gretel. Come sit next to me, little girl," Magnus urged as he chose a spot.

The sauna grew hotter and Hans poured water over the hot rocks before taking a seat on the other side of their Daddy. The three relaxed, feeling their muscles unwind after a long day. Magnus linked his fingers with theirs as they sat there together.

"This is absolutely the second-best gift I've ever been given," Magnus announced.

"The second best?" Gretel said, trying to keep the sadness that statement triggered from echoing in her tone.

"Nothing can beat the gift of finding you and Hans. That is the greatest gift of my life. This sauna is incredible, but it's not the two of you," Magnus explained.

"Oh!" Gretel felt tears fill her eyes with the sweetness of that statement. She turned to kiss Magnus lightly, but that soft touch wasn't enough. Gretel deepened the exchange and felt Hans brush his hand through her hair. She leaned a bit further to kiss Hans as well, and Magnus released her hand to lift her onto his lap.

The heat of the room had coated their skin with sweat. Now huddled together, their hands slid over each other's skin as they exchanged caresses. The sexual tension inside their bodies added extra steam to the room.

Gretel shifted to straddle her Daddy's lap. Magnus divided his time between the two Littles—stroking one manly chest and cupping a soft breast—as he kissed their bodies.

Needing more, Gretel wiggled closer to grind her mound against her Daddy's pelvis. He brushed one hand down her torso to touch her intimately. Gretel gasped at the sensation of his fingers teasing her clit as she moved.

"It's not enough. Please, someone fill me."

"It's time for Gretel to be the peanut butter in our sandwich," Magnus reminded them. "Let's turn you around, Gretel."

Scooping his hands under her knees, Magnus rotated her so that her back faced him. She knelt eagerly on the bench, straddling him as Magnus fitted himself to her drenched opening. His hands guided her down over his thick cock, pressing so deep, Gretel didn't know where her Daddy ended and she began. She bounced experimentally and gasped at the tingles gathering inside her.

Hans's warm mouth closed around her nipple and she groaned from the sensation as both men caressed her. Hans pressed kisses to her slick skin, lowering himself between her knees. Gretel reached over her head to wrap her arms around her Daddy's neck for support as Hans explored her pink folds. Tasting and teasing her with the tip of his tongue and lips, he made the sensations feel almost overwhelming.

Gretel heard Magnus groan and realized that Hans was alternating between tantalizing her and teasing the base of Magnus's thick shaft. Their hands roamed over her body. Losing track of who touched her where, Gretel closed her eyes to focus on the sensations strengthening between her legs.

"Aah!" she shouted into the heated room as her body exploded around Magnus. Her body tightened around him and dragged Magnus into losing his control. When she could catch her breath, Gretel eased herself off Magnus and over to the side.

After pulling her in for a kiss, Magnus shifted to the planking on the floor and patted the bench where he'd previously sat. "Come here, little boy. It's your turn. On your knees."

Eagerly, Hans moved into position in front of Magnus . He held his breath as the older man leaned close to Hans's pelvis. Magnus licked a wide path up Hans's erection, drawing a deep groaning exhale from his Little.

Eager to help, Gretel ran her hands over his torso, teasing here and there where she knew he was sensitive. Her fingers tweaked his nipples as Magnus took his cock into his mouth. When Hans tried to push forward to bury himself in Magnus's mouth, Gretel slapped his bottom.

"Daddy's in charge," she reminded him.

"But, Gretel..." Hans said as his eyes rolled up into his head as Magnus caressed him with his mouth.

"No buts. Daddy's in charge." Shifting behind him now

that her legs could support her, she cupped his buttocks and pulled them slightly apart.

"No, Gretel," Hans pleaded, holding on to Magnus's shoulders for dear life.

"Wet my finger," she insisted, holding her finger to his lips.

When he opened his mouth to refuse, she darted her finger inside. Automatically, his tongue swirled round her fingertip. Hans sucked lightly on her fingers as Gretel squeezed one of his buttocks lightly to remind him where it was going.

Pulling it out of his mouth, Gretel smiled at the pop and the desperate last touch of his tongue. She kissed Hans's shoulder and traced a line down his back to the sensitive skin above his butt. His wiggle made her smile.

Rewetting the fingertip in her mouth, she pulled apart his bottom cheeks again and pressed the tip into the tight ring as Magnus continued to savor him. Pushing in slightly, Gretel could feel Hans's muscles clenching. She loved feeling him react to her touch. Timing her caresses with her Daddy's movements, Gretel watched Hans sway in place. Overwhelmed by the torrent of sensations, he didn't last long.

With a shout, Hans emptied himself into Magnus's mouth. When his Daddy released him, Gretel removed her probing finger. She was thrilled to see Hans was so rocked by the experience that Magnus steadied him as Hans settled onto the bench after their Daddy rose to take a seat between them. Hans and Gretel wrapped their arms around Magnus. She loved the solid strength of the man who'd brought them so much.

"Littles, we need to get out of here for tonight. I don't want to zap your energy too much," Magnus urged when their breath had settled.

Moving slowly, Gretel's muscles felt more relaxed than ever. She allowed Magnus to steer her out into the anteroom, where their clothes waited. Magnus turned the sauna off and patted the control panel after turning it off. Gretel could tell he was enchanted with the gift they had given him. She met Hans's gaze and smiled as he nodded. They had done well.

"Daddy, there's a shower over here to cool off," she said, pointing to the far corner, equipped with a drain and a showerhead.

The cool water felt like ice on their hot bodies. Gretel swore steam came off their skin as they cooled down. When dressed, they moved outside. With their arms wrapped around each other, they walked to their Daddy's big car and he drove them to the rented house.

Movies and snacks for dinner were the perfect plan for the rest of the lazy night. Gretel couldn't wait until they could simply walk across the lawn to stay in the beautiful house. Everything would be perfect then.

# THE END

The movers carried the last of their belongings into the beautiful house. Gretel and Hans had given up their apartment. They hadn't been there since the first night they'd spent with Magnus. He wanted them with him and Magnus knew that they only wanted to be with him.

Standing on the lawn, he looked up at the house that sparkled after Hans and Gretel's loving care had transformed it. He pulled up a picture he'd taken when he'd first spotted the sad, lonely house. From the first moment, Magnus had known that this house still had a lot of living to do. Opening his camera, he took a new photo.

To his delight, when he checked to see if he'd captured a good shot, he discovered two Littles decorated the picture. Hans waved from the corner of the house and Gretel had stepped out the front door. Magnus grinned at the shot. He couldn't have staged it better. The smiles on their faces said everything.

"Hey, you two. Is everything in place?" he called.

"They're setting up the guest bed and then the movers are finished," Gretel assured him.

"Come. Let's take a picture of us and our new home," he said, beckoning them to him.

Hans held his camera because he had the longest arms. The trio laughed as they rotated slightly looking for the perfect shot. Finally, they found it.

"Say cheese," Magnus directed.

"Cheese!" Their voices blended together perfectly.

Within a few minutes, the movers emerged with the last of their equipment to have Magnus sign that they had completed the job. The one with the clipboard looked at the three of them with a curious expression.

"I have to ask. I overheard your names today. You're Hans. You're Gretel. This house looks like it could be made from candy. Are you an evil witch who's planning on eating them?"

Magnus noticed Hans and Gretel avoided looking at each other. "It is a fun world, isn't it when story tales come to life? Thank goodness, that's a sauna in the back and not a huge oven for them to cook me in."

"Oh, wow! The story gets even better. I hope you all live your best lives here. You know... your happily ever after."

"Thank you, sir. Please take this to share with your crew," Magnus said, handing the man a healthy wad of folded money.

"Thank you, sir." With one last look at the house and the inhabitants, the moving supervisor waved the tip in his hand and turned to rejoin the other movers. He obviously shared that they had a big tip for everyone shouted, "Thank you!" as they loaded into the truck.

When it rolled out of sight, Magnus wrapped his arms around their shoulders and guided them toward the house. "There's just one last surprise. You didn't look, did you?"

"No, Daddy," Hans and Gretel answered almost in unison as they shook their heads.

"Very good, littles. I'm glad you followed my instructions. That means you get a very important reward."

"More than getting to see the nursery?" Gretel asked.

"Yes. Let's go. See if you remember where it is. Don't go in until we're all there," he directed.

With a sideways look at each other, Hans and Gretel ran up the stairs to the front door. Magnus was pleased to see Hans open the screen and step back to allow Gretel to enter first. He had such lovely manners and loved Gretel deeply. As he got to the entrance, Magnus could hear them clomping up the stairs. Knowing how long they'd waited, he hurried to join them.

They were bouncing on their toes in restless anticipation as he opened the door. Magnus flipped on the lights and stepped back. They almost fell over each other as they burst into the nursery.

"Wow!" Hans exclaimed.

Gretel was shocked speechless.

The two stood in the middle of the room with their arms wrapped around each other, turning slowly to see everything. "Who painted this?" Hans asked.

"I did. It was a labor of love. I made each brush stroke with hope for our future. It came out very well," Magnus said modestly.

"Well? This is amazing, Daddy," Gretel struggled to say. "You captured the house like it was actually made of candy and even drew Hans and me on the walls next to our cribs."

She walked forward to slide her hand over the beautifully polished oak railing that surrounded the adult-size bed. "There's something in my bed," she cried, squeezing her face against the wooden slats.

"I've got something in mine, too," Hans called with excitement. He tried to reach over and through the railing but couldn't reach it.

"Those are your prizes for being so good. I'll help you," Magnus promised, moving to Hans's crib first. He concealed the secret way to lower the railing as he slid it down. The Littles definitely didn't need to know that.

"How'd you do that?" Gretel asked as she tried to put hers down.

"Daddy's job," Magnus told her as he repeated his actions to disguise the answer.

Distracted by something bright in the crib, Gretel crawled onto the soft mattress and carefully lifted something from her pillow. She glanced over at Hans, who sat cross-legged in his crib with his arms full. His face was buried into a stuffed, red licorice whip. Hugging her stuffie shaped like a wrapped peppermint candy, she inhaled.

"Mine smells like peppermint!" she called.

"Mine smells like red licorice," Hans told her.

"I know you have your stuffie, Snickers, Gretel. But maybe Snickers would like to have a friend," Magnus said, watching her face.

Gretel hid her face and whispered. "I think Snickers will love to have a friend. You don't think we're silly, do you?"

"Silly? You're the sweetest, most talented Littles I've ever met. You each deserve a stuffie to love as much as I love each of you."

Tears poured from Gretel's eyes. Magnus reached in to tug her across the soft comforter and into his arms. At the sound of her sob, Hans slid out of his crib to rush to hers. "Don't cry, Gretel," he urged, wrapping his arms around her.

Magnus wrapped an arm around his Littles and kissed them. "Tell me why you're sad, Gretel."

"I keep thinking this is a dream and I'm going to wake up

and none of it will be true," she mumbled. "Ouch!" she yelped. Her tears stopping immediately. "You didn't have to pinch me, Hans!"

"Anytime you don't believe we're here with Daddy, I'll be glad to test it out for you. This isn't a dream, Gretel. It's not a fairy tale."

Gretel looked at her Daddy, who nodded and added, "You're here with me, safe and free to explore your Little side."

"Okay," Gretel whispered.

Magnus kissed her forehead before asking, "What are you going to name your stuffie, Gretel?"

"Patty, of course."

Hans laughed. That really was the only name for a peppermint candy.

"What are you going to name your red licorice?"

"Nummy," Hans said with a grin. "Because it's so nummy. How did you know I liked red licorice?"

"A little bird might have told me," Magnus confessed.

Hans leaned forward to kiss Gretel lightly. As he leaned back, he bonked Gretel on the nose with Nummy. "Smell!"

Giggling, she inhaled and proclaimed it perfectly licoricey. She returned the favor, allowing Hans to sniff hers.

"That's yummy. Now, I want candy," he declared, looking at his Daddy.

"I think that's my clue to order pizza for dinner tonight. Think they can find our new house?" Magnus asked.

"Just tell them to look for the fairytale house. They can't miss it!" Gretel urged.

Thank you for reading H&G Restorations!!

Don't miss future sweet and steamy Daddy stories by Pepper North? Subscribe to my newsletter!

I'm excited to offer you a glimpse into Drake: Fated Dragon Daddies Book 1. which introduces a centuries-old pact between an ancient town's founders and their powerful allies that could save the inhabitants of their city once again, but only a dragon Daddy can truly guard his mate from harm.

**5.0 out of 5 stars**
**WOW!! So Absorbing!**
Well written story and well developed characters. The book needs to grab me and keep me involved from the beginning and all the way to the end! This one does that very well! I can't wait to read the next one!

**5.0 out of 5 stars**
**Amazing**
It was a fantastic read, loved it would recommend to anyone who likes dragons to give it a read. Pepper did an amazing job as always.

## Drake: Fated Dragon Daddies Book 1
### Chapter One

Aurora quickly walked by the old cemetery. It wasn't that she was afraid of ghosts. She shied away from the activity happening there to give those visiting privacy. Today, a stream of people dressed in black occupied the place. With a glance, Aurora noted someone being buried in one of the old family plots. She shivered at the thought of being locked inside one of the stone mausoleums, even if her family had one.

All the founding families did. They'd established Wyvern centuries ago. The area was sheltered from marauders in a valley surrounded by mountains. Over the years, new settlers had added a ring of newer buildings around the oldest part of the city. It hadn't grown quickly and still held that small, lost-in-time feel.

Cut off from other cities by sheer distance and tricky roads, it was an odd combination of modern living and old-fashioned practices. There was a lot of history in the stone buildings that still formed the center of the town for those who appreciated it—or even stopped to notice the cobbled streets and beastly gargoyles forming the rain spouts of many of the oldest homes and stores.

Just back from finishing her four-year business degree in Dallas, Aurora hadn't been overjoyed to come home with her tail between her legs. She'd been so sure she'd get a job at the elite company she interned for during the summers that she hadn't explored other options. Turned out, the company didn't wish to offer her a position when she graduated, but preferred candidates with five or more years of experience.

She'd scrambled to apply elsewhere but everyone in her graduating class had gotten their applications in first. Aurora wished she had a hundred dollars for every interviewer who told her they wished she had applied earlier but all the positions were now filled. Then she would have been able to pay her rent for a few more months.

The whisper of a noise behind her made her turn. She jumped back at the sight of a stunningly handsome man standing right behind her. His hair was thick—jet black with streaks of silver. It looked slightly unkempt as if he had neglected to cut it for a while. She had the weirdest urge to reach forward and brush it from his eyes.

Clutching her skirt with her hands to avoid giving in to that temptation, Aurora couldn't look away. She shivered slightly at the scar that ran along his cheek. Faded into a white line, it didn't detract from his appeal but gave him a dangerous air, as did the scruffy beard from not shaving for several days. She did not want to mess with this man. Yet, she wondered how his beard would feel if they kissed.

He stretched out a hand and she automatically responded to his silent request. Letting go of the fabric, she placed her palm against his and watched her hand disappear as his powerful one closed around it. A fire flared in his blue eyes, turning them gold. She felt like he could see through her.

Disconcerted, Aurora tried to pull away. She panicked when a sharp heat built on the back of her hand. "You're hurting me," she cried as she tugged harder to free herself.

"I was not expecting to find you today," he said harshly. His statement almost sounded like a curse.

Frightened by his tone, Aurora yanked her hand, trying to free it. He held her effortlessly, not even budging with the force of her movement.

"You will learn that all things happen on my time, Aurora. The pain should be gone now," he commented in a deep voice that seemed to resonate within her.

To her surprise, he abruptly released her hand. She staggered back a few steps, looking at her hand for damage. It was fine. Not a single mark, bruise, or red spot marred her skin. Astonished, she looked up quickly and met his steely gaze.

Aurora was rattled to realize the sharp pain was not the only result of touching him. That reaction soon paled in comparison to a consuming arousal building deep inside her. She'd never felt an attraction like that to anyone. Frightened, Aurora turned and ran down the cobbled streets of the Old Town.

She looked back over her shoulder before turning the corner and found him still standing there watching her. Feeling as if she were physically dragging herself away, Aurora dashed to her car and threw herself inside. Driving away felt awful for a few blocks before the need to turn around ebbed slightly—still there, but less urgent.

The heat, however, didn't abate. All she could think about was getting home to spend time with her vibrator. A picture of the room she shared with her sister once again popped into her mind. Aurora shook her head. There simply was no privacy in the home she shared with her family. There would be no relief for her there.

Gritting her teeth, she continued driving. Her family's home was in the middle of the modernized section of Wyvern surrounding the oldest section of the city. Her grandparents still occupied the ancestral home in the Old Town. It was large and had many rooms for guests. They would welcome her to stay with them.

Making a decision quickly, Aurora pulled onto a side street and parked. She pulled her phone out of her purse and called her grandmother.

"Hi, Aurora. I'm so glad to hear from you. Have you changed your mind? Can I tempt you to come stay with us?"

"Hi, Grandma. Like always, you can read my mind. I think sometimes you know me better than I do."

"There is a tie between all the women of our lineage," her grandmother said knowingly.

Not knowing what to say to that, Aurora concentrated on her reason for calling. "I did call to see if I can live with you for a while. Just until I find a job. Then, I'm afraid I'll have to move away from Wyvern."

"There's plenty of time to worry about the future. I'm going to focus on today. Believe it or not, Madelyn freshened up the pink room for you today. I had a feeling you might be coming soon."

Aurora smiled. The crafty woman knew she loved the ruffles and lace in the beautiful room. "You are the best, Grandma. I'm going to go pack some things and I'll be there in a couple hours."

"We'll be glad to see you, sweetheart."

Smiling, Aurora disconnected the call and dropped her phone in her purse. She merged back into traffic. Her grandparents would hover and be interested in everything she did. Even as an adult, she'd need to be home by a reasonable hour. That wasn't a problem. She'd gotten burned out on partying in college and she definitely didn't have a boyfriend to spend the night with.

Just that thought of having sex made her hunch over slightly as the heat inside her flared. *What in the hell is going on?* She'd had sex before but didn't really understand the allure.

Sex was okay, but she'd never seen rockets bursting in the air. The guys she'd been with seemed to think it was her fault she hadn't orgasmed. Whatever they were doing seemed to work for other girls. Either she was weird in some way, or their previous partners had totally faked their orgasms. Aurora was betting the second one was the truth.

She pressed a hand low on her abdomen, trying to soothe the ache. Never had she felt anything like this, even at the beginning of a relationship when she'd been the most attracted to her boyfriend at the time. Maybe something was wrong.

Shaking her head at the mere thought of going to the doctor, she abandoned that plan. How in the world would she explain this feeling to a doctor? She'd go if it didn't get better in a few days. Maybe she just ate something that was off.

When she pulled up in the drive, her sister rushed out to meet her.

"You can't put your stuff on my side of the room," Sheila informed her as Aurora got out of the car.

"Sorry. I didn't mean to invade." Distracted by a thick tower of black smoke at the top of one of the mountains surrounding the city, she wondered if the fire would endanger Wyvern.

"And yet you always do," Sheila sneered, drawing her back into the conversation. "Your laundry basket is one inch over in my space."

"Yikes. I'll move it," Aurora promised. She knew her sister had thoroughly enjoyed having the room to herself when Aurora had gone to college. It was hard to lose that independence. "Grandma called and I'm going to stay with them for a while."

"Really?" Sheila tried unsuccessfully to keep the excitement out of her voice.

"Really. Try not to miss me too bad," Aurora urged, walking inside and holding the door open for her sister.

"Why should she miss you?" Aurora's father, Carl, asked.

"She's going to stay at Grandma's," Sheila rushed to tell him.

"That's a great idea. They'll love to have you there," her father said with a smile. "You do know you're always welcome here, despite what your kid sister might have said."

"Hey! I didn't say anything," Sheila protested.

"Sheila's been great. It seemed like a good idea to spend time with Grandma and Grandpa before I move away for a job. They're not getting any younger," Aurora pointed out.

"They're going to be around for a while," her dad said with a laugh. "But I think you'll both enjoy having each other around." He didn't have to add, 'unlike your sister who's counting down the days until you leave.'

A flare of desire caught her by surprise, and she pressed a hand to her stomach.

"Ew! You're not getting sick, are you?" Sheila asked with all the drama a sixteen-year-old could muster.

"Nope. I'm good. I'll just go grab my stuff."

In the shared bedroom, she quickly packed clothes she would need for the next couple of weeks. She could always come back for more if she got tired of wearing them. Even under the watchful eye of her sister, she was able to get the one thing she needed most into her suitcase. She crossed her fingers that the vibrator would ease the need growing inside her.

When she picked up her childhood stuffie, Sheila made fun of her. "Don't you think it's time you gave up your stuffed animal? How many college graduates still sleep with one every night?"

"Firefly will be with me forever. Some friends are for life."

Aurora had known upon seeing the stuffie that he was hers. She'd always been a compliant child, not one who used tantrums to get her way. That day remained in her memory as clear as day. She could not leave without Firefly and had sat down in the middle of the aisle with the stuffie pressed to her heart. Finally, her father had given her an advance on her allowance to buy him. Aurora hadn't cared a bit about losing her spending money. Firefly was worth that and more.

Pushing her sister's teasing from her mind, Aurora checked her closet for anything else she needed to take with her. She ran through the things she knew she'd need. Jeans, check. Leggings, check. T-shirts, check. Underwear, check. *Hmmm, I might need some fancier clothes.*

Scrutinizing her choices, Aurora picked out a pair of slacks and a white button-down shirt. As a lark, she grabbed the short black cocktail dress she'd worn to bars. It was nice enough that if her grandparents had a dinner party she could dress for the event.

Walking out the front door, she lugged everything to her sensible sedan. All that remained was to hug everyone goodbye and make sure she had her charger.

"Hey, Dad. On my way out. Do you know where Mom is?" Aurora asked, bracing her hand on the leather recliner next to the twin that held her father.

"What's that on your hand?" he asked.

Bemused, she held out her right hand, palm up. Maybe he was going to give her some money. To her surprise, he turned it over to look at the normally smooth skin on top of her hand. There were some raised bumps on it. He stroked a finger over one small section.

"Eccch!" She yanked her hand away and slapped it over her mouth as a wave of overwhelming nausea almost made her throw up.

"I thought you said you weren't sick?" her sister taunted from the entrance to the hallway.

"Talk to my mom about your hand," her father said quietly. Looking more serious than she'd seen him before, he pulled Aurora into his arms and hugged her tightly before releasing her. "Go on. You can call your mom later and explain."

"Thanks, Dad."

Aurora fled through the front door and gulped fresh air desperately. The nausea abated quickly. Jumping into her car, she turned on the radio to distract herself and drove away. Maybe she was sick. Grandma would know what to do. She always knew.

Her eyes automatically went to the mountain in front of her. The smoke had lessened. Whatever it was, it looked like it would not be a threat now.

Want to read more? One-click Drake: Fated Dragon Daddies Book 1!

READ MORE **from Pepper North**

**Devil Daddies**

The members of the Devil Daddies MC will risk all to secure two things: special acquisitions and women with a Little side.ly guard his mate from harm.

**Fated Dragon Daddies**

Change is coming to Wyvern.
A centuries-old pact between the founders and their powerful allies could save the inhabitants of the city once again, but only a dragon Daddy can truly guard his mate from harm.

## Shadowridge Guardians

Combining the sizzling talents of bestselling authors Pepper North, Kate Oliver, and Becca Jameson, the Shadowridge Guardians are guaranteed to give you a thrill and leave you dreaming of your own throbbing motorcycle joyride.

Are you daring enough to ride with a club of rough, growly, commanding men? The protective Daddies of the Shadowridge Guardians Motorcycle Club will stop at nothing to ensure the safety and protection of everything that belongs to them: their Littles, their club, and their town. Throw in some sassy, naughty, mischievous women who won't hesitate to serve their fair share of attitude even in the face of looming danger, and this brand new MC Romance series is ready to ignite!

## Danger Bluff

Welcome to Danger Bluff where a mysterious billionaire brings together a hand-selected team of men at an abandoned resort in New Zealand. They each owe him a marker. And they all have something in common—a dominant shared code to nurture and protect. They will repay their debts one by one, finding love along the way.

**A Second Chance For Mr. Right**

For some, there is a second chance at having Mr. Right. Coulda, Shoulda, Woulda explores a world of connections that can't exist... until they do. Forbidden love abounds when these Daddy Doms refuse to live with regret and claim the women who own their hearts.

## Little Cakes

Welcome to Little Cakes, the bakery that plays Daddy matchmaker! Little Cakes is a sweet and satisfying series, but dare to taste only if you like delicious Daddies, luscious Littles, and guaranteed happily-ever-afters.

### Dr. Richards' Littles®

A beloved age play series that features Littles who find their forever Daddies and Mommies. Dr. Richards guides and supports their efforts to keep their Littles happy and healthy.

Note: Zoey; Dr. Richards' Littles® 1 is available FREE on Pepper's website:
4PepperNorth.club

Dr. Richards' Littles®
is a registered trademark of
With A Wink Publishing, LLC.
All rights reserved.

## SANCTUM

Pepper North introduces you to an age play community that is isolated from the surrounding world. Here Littles can be Little, and Daddies can care for their Littles and keep them protected from the outside world.

**Soldier Daddies**

What private mission are these elite soldiers undertaking? They're all searching for their perfect Little girl.

## The Keepers

This series from Pepper North is a twist on contemporary age play romances. Here are the stories of humans cared for by specially selected Keepers of an alien race. These are science fiction novels that age play readers will love!

## The Magic of Twelve

The Magic of Twelve features the stories of twelve women transported on their 22nd birthday to a new life as the droblin (cherished Little one) of a Sorcerer of Bairn. These magic wielders have waited a long time to take complete care of their droblin's needs. They will protect their precious one to their last drop of magic from a growing menace. Each novel is a complete story.

Ever just gone for it? That's what *USA Today* Bestselling Author Pepper North did in 2017 when she posted a book for sale on Amazon without telling anyone. Thanks to her amazing fans, the support of the writing community, Mr. North, and a killer schedule, she has now written more than 180 books! Enjoy contemporary, paranormal, dark, and erotic romances that are both sweet and steamy? Pepper will convert you into one of her loyal readers. What's coming in the future? A Daddypalooza!

Sign up for Pepper North's newsletter

Like Pepper North on Facebook

Join Pepper's Readers' Group for insider information and giveaways!

Follow Pepper everywhere!
Amazon Author Page
BookBub
FaceBook
GoodReads
Instagram
TikToc
Twitter
YouTube
Visit Pepper's website for a current checklist of books!

Printed in Dunstable, United Kingdom